The Time Traveler's Wife

CSM Publishing
Araraquara, Brazil 2015
Second Edition

All artwork and layout by C. Sean McGee
Copy Editing by AnnaVanti
Woman Photo: Victor Tongdee

ISBN 13 - 978-1502926425

ISBN 10 - 1502926423

C. Sean McGee

The Time Traveler's Wife

contents

1.6180339887498948482045868343656381177203 0917980576286213544862270526046281890.......	9
Through the Wormhole of Sudden Applause	21
A Brief Introduction to Active Noise Reduction	31
Increment IV – licks, grooves, sweeps and tasty fills	41
If the Mouth is the Asshole of the Subconscious Mind, What then of the Sound of My Thoughts?	51
A Bushel of Salt	74

for nenagh and tomás

1.61803398874989484820458 8343656381177203091798.......

"You ever driven all night, really tired? You know, so tired that even if were to crash, you probably wouldn't even feel a thing anyway? And then you get home or wherever the hell you're going and you take the keys out of the ignition and you think to yourself, 'how the fuck did I get here?' You can't remember a bit of the journey. You were asleep or dreaming the whole time or something. You don't know if you leaned into any of the turns and you can't be sure or not if you ran over an animal or a mother pushing a pram across the street. The only thing you know is that you're pretty sure this is where you're supposed to be; home or work or the supermarket. You just, can't remember for the life of you, how you got here. You ever felt that?"

"Sure. I try not to drive tired, on account of it being so dangerous, but yeah" Stefan said, sipping his Mocha, "I once drove through the night when I was in university with some friends you know, back in the days where you're reckless and living like there's no tomorrow. So anyway, we...."

"I feel that way about my life," John said, twisting his cup back and forth, his cold and untouched coffee spilling in a single line down over his index finger and onto the table.

Stefan was waving at a group of guys who had just piled off a coach and were slapping each other's backs and high fiving one another as they joked out loud about celebrities they'd love to fuck and how they'd do it to them. None of them seemed to notice, but that didn't matter to Stefan. He kept waving anyway as if they had as if it was just their way and he made a strange gesture with his fingers to no one in particular as if he were asking for two of something.

"So who would you fuck?" he asked, turning back to John.

"I don't know man. Whoever."

"No, seriously. Let's say you could fuck whoever you wanted

and you could fuck them whatever way you wanted and they weren't you know, gonna make you feel dirty about it or nothing. Who would you fuck? How would you do it?"

John and Stefan sat on the steps to the office building. Neither of them was in the way of passing workers but Stefan's lingering stare and twitching ear grasped the lapels of busied and personal discourse, silently begging, like the basketball player nobody wants, to be picked to give his opinion, to share his thoughts and to laugh as heartily as he saw the other guys doing.

"I can't remember a single choice I ever made," said John, now shaking the cup so that the cold coffee stormed like a raging sea. "I mean, I know who I am and I know what I do. I know what I have to do and for what I have to do, up to now, I know exactly what I've done and what I've still yet to do. And I know when it's gonna be done. I just don't know how the fuck I came to this point. I don't know if I decided all of this or if it just settled around me while I was sleeping or something."

"I'd fuck Jennifer Connelly. She has this natural beauty, you know? Seductive and shapely but natural at the same time. Not many women have that. Like she could be your neighbour or teaching your kid in school and yet at the same time, she has this super sexy side with massive tits and you just know she'd make you cum in a second. Yeah, I'd definitely fuck Jennifer Connelly. I don't think I'd want to do anything nasty, though. Probably just hold her or something. Spoon maybe."

"I think I'm suicidal, but I'm not sure."

"But if I did have to have nasty sex. I don't know. Oprah maybe. Early nineties Oprah though. Frizzy hair, sugar on her fingers. No, wait, Ricki Lake. She was fucking hot, even when she was chubby. Can I bang two?" Stefan asked, looking at John with genuine concern rasping his brow.

John was staring at his reflection on the tips of his shoes. He always kept them at such a shine and his pants, they were never wrinkled and were ironed just right, so the pleats stuck out like the fold in his favourite novel. His shirt was a little big for him, but he tucked the length of it into his pants and lightly tugged on it so the fold hung in a cool and professional manner over his buckle.

And his tie, it was the only one he had ever bought. It cost him nearly a hundred dollars at the time. It was silk, and the colour and pattern made it look like someone had spilt extravagant art down his neck and along his chest. Its colour was faded now and its texture was coarse; its fibres splitting into ugly tufts, looking less like a piece of art and more like a shitty sketch, etched on the back of a soiled napkin.

"We live and we die," said John.

"If I could fuck them both, I'd probably fuck Ricki Lake in the ass and I'd lay Oprah on Ricki Lake's back like a tablecloth and I'd just eat that early nineties pussy," Stefan said, blowing raspberries into his hand as he mocked his ravenous sexual appetite. "And I'd have to have Donahue commentating. He could be in the back, jerking off and talking about how big my cock is. But I don't know" he said, perplexed. "I don't if I'd cum in Ricki Lake's asshole or on Oprah's tits or if I'd try and shoot on their faces you know. That would be hot."

"I think maybe I'm depressed," said John.

"God. Lighten up It's called 'Who Would You Fuck?' Not 'How to be a Kill Joy'. What's gotten into you anyway? You're normally a lot more chipper than this. You're so…"

"Choose your next words carefully," John thought, imagining himself taking Stefan by a clump of his hair and beating his face against the rounded edge of the red-bricked stairs.

"The opposite of full of life," he said, between sips of his Mocha, not noticing the twitch and tremor in John's eye as he stared at the different groups of guys and gals coming off of buses and coaches and piling out of cars. "Today's gonna be a good day, I can tell. I can feel it."

"I don't care."

"We're gonna get our bonuses. Just in time too. Have you seen the cost of sliced pepperoni? It's daylight robbery I'm telling you. That and the cost of socks, which the kids just tear holes through every second they get. You'll see when you and Tracy to stop kidding around of course. You'll see what I mean. Have you talked about it much? I mean, does she want kids?"

"I don't know," said John.

"What about you? One, two, four?" Stefan scoffed.

"I don't care."

"But I tell you, John," Stefan said, hardly listening, "if the bonus comes through… You know… Everything kind of evens out and…"

"Stays exactly the same," John said, spilling his cold coffee to the floor, watching the black liquid trickle over the edge of the step and cascade onto the bowing weed below.

"Exactly. If it ain't broke…"

Both men picked themselves up and made their way into the foyer and then crowded by the elevator with Stefan pricking his ears to the tune of the current theme. Although they mostly worked on separate floors, the suited workers were always engaged in such delicate debate as if they had scholarly or juvenile ties, going from political polemic to that shit hot new song from Nine Inch Nails, the house remix, not the original, and why wearing white speedos was no longer gay.

"So what did you guys get up to on the weekend?"

He was talking to John, but Stefan's voice and attention travelled around the elevator carrying into the creeps of whispered conversations, trying to make its presence pertinent.

"Nothing really," said John.

He tried to think, not for the sake of Stefan but for his own curiosity. What had he done? Had he really done nothing or was this just something he had become accustomed to saying?

On Friday, he and Tracy watched a movie. They hadn't seen it before, but everyone was raving about it. It was a copy of a copy of a copy and he couldn't remember if he enjoyed it or not, or if he had seen the original. The actors were all famous though so at worst; it would have been comfortable to be around people he knew even if, in the movie, nothing much happened.

"Yeah us too. You know. Once you get kids everything really gets set in stone. It's like finding your north as if one day some guy comes up to you and hands you a compass and then everything makes sense. You have your direction. Up at seven, take the kids to practice, and back for lunch. Mow the lawn. Eat. Get into trimming the hedges. Oh, I spoke to Jeff my neighbour; he popped his head over the fence the rascal. That was unexpected. Yeah, he's pretty much the same. So then in the afternoon, my littlest wanted to…"

He carried on like this for the entire ride. He must take notes. He'd have to. No one could remember all that. Maybe he was just used to it. After all, he'd had the same weekend for the last eight years. If he didn't know off by heart know, well….

"See, I don't know if I'm bored or I'm upset. I don't know. I never learned this at school. I learned how to do so much shit that I'll never have the capacity, the chance or the fucking will to do. I know how a crane works. I can peel a potato eight different ways and I'm a little more than average at playing Green sleeves on a recorder. I can speak French, Dutch, Mandarin, Portuguese and English. I can read and write in eleven types of computer code. I can even unhook a bra. Yet, I can't tell the difference between being bored and depressed. And If I am bored then I just need to do something. I just need to keep myself busy. But if I'm depressed and the things I'm doing are making me feel this way, then at the end of the day, I'm only gonna feel worse. So I don't know what to do."

"This weekend?" asked Stefan, louder than before. "Well, come over," he said, having assumed the gist of John's admission. "We're having a barbeque for Thanksgiving."

"You always have a barbeque for Thanksgiving," John said, picking at a rough hair poking out of his nose. "And I'm always there. And I sit in the same god damned seat below that stupid mosquito killer and, know LED doesn't attract mosquitos right?"

Stefan was trawling the other guys and gals, seeing if anyone was nibbling at his bait.

"And we always eat the same five buck steaks and the sausages always have charcoaled ends. And we spend the whole night talking about how things were and then we settle on the fact that

that's ok. That it's fine, that we'll never get to think or act or feel that way again. And then you tell me about your fucking kids and you force one of them to do some retarded fucking dance that you can tell they are not comfortable in fucking doing man, but you push them. And probably by themselves, they get it but who gives a fuck, that doesn't matter. Fact is, you get drunk and tell them to do that funny thing and to do that dance, that dance they do. And they fuck it up, and you laugh royally, and they cringe and squirm like dry shrivelled sponges, and you open another beer, and the sausages start to burn, and then at some point, I get the courage to say fuck it, we have to go."

"Of course, you have to go," said Stefan, catching only the last words. "Anyway, you gotta see this thing the kids have been working on. It's ace. It really is. I swear, now I know most parents say this, but my girl, she has talent you know."

The elevator opened on the top floor, The Dairy Parlor. All of the workers were there, gathered in their departments and their teams, bunched up together, gossiping and laughing as Managers, dressed in gumboots and yellow raincoats, kneeled before each person, attaching wires with small electrodes to each person's cheeks and sneakily, under their garments, to the tips of their nipples.

And in the laps of each person, The Managers placed reading paraphernalia. For some, it was a newspaper filled with headlines of war and disparity. In others, they placed thick plastic books with short, simple to follow stories of playing pets and busy farm animals and with mounds of fur and brushy hair, for the reader to stroke, before they turned each page.

John fidgeted as the electrodes were placed on his nipples; the cold, or maybe his boredom making him uncomfortable. When he moved, The Manager let go of the clamp and it bit down hard on his shrinking nipple and he screamed.

"Watch it" he shouted.

The Manager said nothing. They never did. He just realigned the clamp and called in another manager to hold John still so that they could finish getting him prepared. They had so much work to do after all.

As he sat in his cubicle, the electrodes lightly stimulated his left nipple causing his thoughts to flurry, John sat still, watching a television screen in front of him but not watching it at all. There was a video playing of his thoughts and there was a device besides the television that was recording everything. And from one of his nipples, his creativity oozed in a thick creamy liquid from a thin transparent tube that curled around his body and his chair and fed into a silver bucket that rattled with every drop.

"We're planning our next vacation," said Stefan, his screen showing a video of a group of armed Jihadists, synchronized dancing. "October, '32"

"You realize that's decades away right?"

"You book in early, you get the best rates. Prior preparation prevents poor performance, Doug."

"It's John."

"Exactly. You have to know what you're doing so you can do it well. So you don't have to think about what you're doing. You can think about whatever you want."

"That's why I can't remember anything. Not that it matters."

"Everything matters. That's why we do it."

"I don't need to remember anything because nothing ever changes. Everything is the same. This" John said, looking at his cubicle and realizing that he had spent almost half his life in here, being milked daily of his thoughts and his ideas.

"This what?" Stefan asked, his screen now showing a football match and two dogs mating, in the corner of the goal square.

"We do the same thing every day. We come here. We sit in this stall. We get milked and for what? Where does it go?"

"In the bucket," Stefan said.

"And then what? Our ideas are mixed, watered down and pasteurized and then packaged and labelled and branded and sold to some other poor schmuck in some other city in some other part of the world. He drinks our Creative Milk and we drink his. So what's the point?"

"It's your job. Stop analyzing things. Anyway, you can't drink your own Creative Milk. It's not good for you. Maybe if you were like on a desert island or something. But…" he said, making a disgusted face. "I couldn't," he said, shaking his head and tongue protruding like a poisoned cat.

"Do you think about dying at all?" John asked, his television screen now looking like a mirror, showing his pale reflection looking back at him, frowning miserably.

"Me? I can't see the point. The wife does. I don't really pay much mind. It doesn't faze me. You'd have to get her roots under a microscope to find her true colour. Not my thing, though."

"We live and we die," John said, the image on his screen showing just a grain of sand. "That's it. The most significant event in my life is my death. And everything else…."

"I wanted to do something different but then, why take the risk? So we're thinking of going with the same resort. If it ain't broke…"

"If every day in my life is the same if one week is no different to the last then what's the point?" John said, peering around his cubicle wall into Stefan's. "If there's nothing new, if there are no more synapses, if I can't taste cumin again for the first time, if I can't ever taste cold on my tongue again for the first time, if I can't feel or fuck or speak like it fucking matters, then what's the point? If I have already defined every dimension of my every sense if there are no more surprises, then why delay the inevitable? Why shouldn't I kill myself now?"

"You should have kids."

"What the fuck will that prove?"

"It'll even you out. Be critical of someone else, takes the focus off yourself."

The image on John's screen was now of a house that he used to live next to when he was just a boy. The image was fuzzy, just like it was in his thoughts. The memory had been with him his whole life, that of gathering at the steps of this building each October and running for dear life with the other children as from within the house, a dark impervious figure with a black cloak and sharp-fanged teeth took flight from the doorway and chased the children down the street.

He had few memories of when he was a boy but those that he did have, they now played out on the screen before him. There was Dracula, his neighbour, and how tried to kill all of the children and how nobody, not even his own mother and father, ever said a thing.

And then, the memory of watching his friends all climb onto the sinking mound of mud of dirt in the adjacent park and wishing he could but feeling trapped, as on the screen and in his thoughts, the young boy in his memories stared down at the bright red skates that he wore on his feet, the reason he couldn't climb that mound.

"What did you want to be when you were young?"

"I wanted to be a Manager," Stefan said. "Of anything really. Just a Manager. What about you?"

On Stefan's screen, there was the image that he had in his mind. It was the image of himself, standing in yellow Wellington's and a yellow raincoat with a floppy yellow hat. His pants sat high on his waist and his belt, which was nothing more than the cord of an old toaster, was tied into one thick knot and its loose end hanged down past his knees. He didn't look happy but then again, most Managers never really were. He carried a clump of lettuce in one hand which he was feeding to a worker in their cubicle and in his other hand he carried a silver bucket full to the brim of thick creamy Creative Milk.

"I didn't want to be anything," John said. "And that's the thing. I didn't know what anything was, so I never imagined what I would ever want to be. And I wanna feel that way again. I don't wanna know what the weather is gonna be like for the next ten fucking days. I don't wanna plan my fucking vacation. I don't wanna live in the future, not anymore. I don't want to go through life content, feeling nothing, feeling so god damn secure. No love, no fear. I don't want repetition. I don't want consistency. I want surprise. I want change. I want discord. I want to feel what it's like to drive on the wrong side of the street, to write with my wrong hand and to feel as if nothing is certain as if there is no future as if now is vital as if the present is all that matters."

"Is something the matter John?"

It was his Manager, sitting on a wooden stool beside him, massaging John's nipple between his thick burly fingers and lifting the near-empty silver bucket to his face.

"Is everything right at home? Is there anything you need to

talk about? You know I did a course in Occupational Health so if you need to, you know, just talk, we can take a minute away from the milking and you can, you know, make up the time at the end of the day. But this" he said, swirling the few drops at the bottom of the silver bucket. "This is unacceptable."

"Fire me," John said. "Please."

"Well," said The Manager pensive, "Let's not go down that path just yet. We do have an action plan, though."

John imagined himself revolting, thrusting his clenched fist into his Manager's smiling face but it was no use. His head was made of jelly and though it wobbled about, it didn't, as he had hoped, fall off of his shoulders.

"Can I change department then? I think I'd like a change. I need a change."

"I'll see what I can do," The Manager said, struggling to get up from the tiny stool before walking down the hallway with the empty silver bucket in his hands.

"You ever wish you'd done things differently? Or what would happen, if you had? If you could go back, what would you change?"

"Hold on buddy. Trying to concentrate. Nearly done here. And…" Stefan said, drawing his last word with the last drops of milk from his swollen nipple into his now full and nearly overflowing silver bucket.

John peered out from his cubicle. Down along the rows of small office spaces, he could see his fellow colleagues all unclamping their nipples and ejecting their video cassettes from the VCRs that sat adjacent to their monitors. They seemed to enjoy their work. Most looked relieved like they had just finished a marathon. Some joked lightly as they stacked their cassettes, making light of the poor weather and last night's upset. Most were cynical, quite adamant that The Team never had a chance in the first place. No one at all seemed surprised or even upset by the result.

John hated football. Not for the sport itself, but for the social obligation. Listening, though, to the murmurs about him, he quickly realized that how they felt about the upset was how he had felt about himself. It was how he had felt about his life, about his job, about his thinning hair and his flabby body. It was how he had felt about the size of his penis and about the tufts of grey hair that had just recently sprouted in his nose. It was how he had felt about the things he had wanted to do his whole life but had never gotten around to. It was how he had felt about his garden and his scabby cat and it was how he had felt about his wife.

It was how he had felt, until now.

And then, as quickly as his colleagues had packed their cassettes into hardcover casings, each unwrapped one more, loading them into the VCRs before reattaching the cold steel clamps to their nipples and starting another task; the filling of another silver pail.

Most had seventeen cassettes piled on top of one another. It was an average, what was expected by working at an average capacity. John looked around at his workstation. His table was empty except for a Diet Coke and a picture of his wife, from when she was younger before he knew her. She didn't know that he kept that photo and he'd probably never tell her. And though it seemed innocuous, keeping this exact picture, it felt like something that she wouldn't understand.

He sat there staring at the picture of the woman he never knew and he imagined what she was like before the first time that he saw her, before the first time she turned to him and her sight was littered with his attention, before her thoughts were corrupted and polluted with his image, before they finished each other's sentences, when it was that she had a complete and independent thought of her own.

He sat there staring at the picture and beside him; he had not one packed cassette.

"Come with me John," The Manager said. He sounded serious. He even remembered his name.

"Am I being fired?"

Though he wanted it, all he could think of were the seven remaining instalments for the outdoor setting they had bought last September but had never used. Then he thought about his wife and how upset she would be and then, how upset that would make him.

And he hated himself, for making himself feel that way.

"You're being promoted," The Manager said.

John's eyes widened. He'd been expecting a raise, everyone had; something small and trivial that would take the edge off the rising interest rates on his backdated loans.

"Congratulations," The Manager said, pointing to a cubicle at the end of the row. "You've been promoted to Team Coordinator. You must be pleased. You deserve it."

John stepped into the cubicle. He looked around. It was cramped just like his old cubicle. And the chair where he would sit, its air compressed handle had its rounded plastic end broken, just like his last chair. And there was a monitor just like his old monitor and a VCR too. And on the ground were a small beige stool and an empty silver pail, waiting to be filled, just like his old cubicle.

He tucked his head around the side and peered into the next cubicle and he saw Stefan, filling another pail, thinking about Monster Trucks and smiling as he shook his extended thumb maddeningly as if he were trying to shake off a serious burn.

"I don't get it," John said. "I thought I was promoted? Nothing changed. I'm in the same cubicle."

He wanted to shout the word fuck. He wanted to say that it was exactly the fucking same. He wanted to emphasize that, to shout the word fucking. He wanted to offend The Manager, for him to feel like he felt now. He wanted to, but he didn't.

"Congratulations," The Manager said, clapping loudly and inciting the whole office into a massive lauding roar.

"Bravo," they all shouted. "Bravo. We wish we were you."

John stared idly at his cubicle and then at the picture of his wife.

"Would you like me to massage your nipples?" The Manager asked.

"No thanks," John said politely. "I can do it myself."

Through the Wormhole of Sudden Applause

"You know what I love?" Stefan asked, loosening his tie and sniffing the air as if the blurring luminescence were gently swaying pine.

"Going home" John replied.

"Going home. That's right. Going home. How did you know I was going to say that?"

"That's all you ever say at the end of every day."

"Still," Stefan said, now pulling his oversized white shirt from beneath his straining beltline. "It feels good to be going home."

In the elevator, Stefan, along with the men from the other floors, talked about what show he was going to watch tonight after the news and the football and then a debate broke out about what our role was in the Middle East and one of the men, in particular, he seemed to have just the right thing to say about every issue. Not everyone was impressed, but that didn't mean they didn't concede their opinion and like an infant lulling itself to sleep, gasp resignedly, accepting that they had no voice, none that could be heard anyway.

As they hammered on about political affairs, naming cruel dictators and Neo-Fascist Fundamentalist Regimes, John couldn't help but stare at a spider in the upright corner of the elevator. He or she was no different to the monsters being berated by young men with cheap suits and sore nipples. For, like the dictator, the spider kept a kind of unnerving state of balance and order. Though there was potential for the spider to swing low and bite at the neck of some unsuspecting Western liberal, the truth was, it was more interested in collecting tiny blood-sucking insects for its lunch and its pleasure. And like the dictator, if the spider was ever removed from power, if some fearful liberating sponge were to wipe away its sticky veil of authority, there would be no order anymore and all of those blood-sucking insects, they would be free to bite, suck and wreak havoc in this humid cramped space.

John feared the spider, but he was thankful that it was there.

The elevator stopped on the seventh floor and a pretty girl got on. She had long straight black hair that was tied in a ponytail which was pulled so tight that not a single hair was out of place. She wore bright red glasses and purple lipstick and she had a tattoo of a naked woman, straddling a mechanical phallus. The tattoo started on her neck, just below her ear and it ran all the way down her left arm. The last of it, the pointed tail of some winged reptile, curled onto the palm of her hand.

The workers all retreated into an awkward silence, some tucking their heaving stomachs closer to their expanding waistlines, feigning general disinterest but watching, with a sharp peripheral eye on the strange pretty girl who was both demure and dangerous, efficacious and meek, to see if she was wetted to their staunch masculine physique.

She stood beside John humming a song that he hadn't heard in such a long time. He couldn't remember which the song was; only that he had loved it once, just as this girl probably did now. The girl smiled at John, but he didn't notice. He was travelling through his thoughts, trying to find the name of that song.

On the way to the car, Stefan was talking about his children's performances at school and how being a father was so clichéd but that the thing about clichés was, they were true, that's why they were clichés. Not because they were uneducated guesses at thoughts and feelings and at social conditions, but because they were ubiquitous and common and absolutely sure and right, and that's what made clichés, clichés.

Stefan was happy about this.

John on the other hand…

Stefan continued talking about his life and then about which girls in the office he would love to fuck and the carnal and depraved acts they would no doubt beg of him to inflict upon them. And he swung his words and swagger like a nymph would, their veiny and stiffened erection, thrusting his hips back and forth and flicking his tongue between the extended V of his fingers. John wondered if

Stefan had even seen his penis in the last ten years. So much fat and matted pubic hair hung over that he was sure Stefan must piss in the shower, so as not to make a mess.

"It's all about the V," Stefan said.

"Why didn't your parents call you Steven?" John asked. "Was it like a Pseudo-European thing?"

As he responded, John saw that girl again, and as Stefan spoke, walking towards John's car, John verged off in the direction of the girl, baited, not by a sexing desire, but by a hint of the past, a time that he had wished away when he was living it and now – now that time was like a pail of bricks that he carried on his shoulders, the past was somewhere where he longed to return.

"Hey, John," Stefan shouted, standing by John's car and shrugging his shoulders excessively as if he didn't understand the situation. "I don't understand," he said, confirming.

John ignored his friend and his colleague, someone he had, like a meaningless popular expression, learned to understand and even appreciate over the years but as of late, someone that he despised and someone who he daydreamed about in an explicit and violent manner.

"You're going the wrong way" Stefan shouted. "The car is here."

What the fuck was she humming? He knew what it was. It was right there on the tip of his tongue. But what was it? What the fuck was it? And how far back had she taken him?

"I'll see you tonight then."

He ignored Stefan and followed the girl through the car park and onto the sidewalk and then down along the avenue until they reached the bus stop. There he stood just behind her and he listened to her humming, closing his eyes and letting his mind wander, trying not to determine what the song was but instead, to let his subconscious decide for him, just as it had every other moment of his life, decided upon innocuous little things like what cold tasted like on the tip of his tongue, the edges of his teeth and on the roof of his mouth. And on whether he should piss straight into the bowl with arrogant disregard for how his guests feel or whether he should gyrate in quiet and careful circles and run the risk of missing the bowl entirely and pissing on the floor. And so, listening to the girl hum, he let his subconscious decide for him just as he had let it decide upon following her in the first place.

The bus came and he got on, following the girl but with a person or two between them, so she wouldn't become suspicious and stop her humming. When he paid the fare to the driver he turned in the direction of the seats but the girl was gone. He tried looking left and right, but he couldn't see her anywhere. It was as if she never got on.

Then who was he following?

"Hurry up mister," spoke a person behind, pushing against his back and urging him down the aisle.

The thought of getting off only came when it was too late when he was already wedging himself in the aisle, pushing his way down the back of the bus. The doors closed and the bus driver honked his horn and then after a shaky start, the bus made its way onto the freeway.

John scanned the bus looking for the girl, but all he could see was the same sight. Seat after seat and row after row, he saw scores of people huddled together and sitting cramped and uncomfortable next to each other, all with the same book tied to their faces, all with the covers facing out with their fingers moving over every word as they all read in thorough enjoyment, the blurb on the backs of their books. John moved down the aisle bewildered by what he saw. And it wasn't until he got near the middle of the bus that he saw an empty seat that nobody had bothered to fill and so he sat down.

There was a young man sitting by the window reading a book with no cover. John sat beside him and at first tried to keep his attention from floating back to the man's book, but he couldn't resist.

"What are you reading?" he asked.

"A book," The Man said.

"That's obvious. What's it called?"

The Man turned to the coverless plank front page. He shook

his shoulders and went back to reading.

"Has no title?" he said.

"Every book has a title."

"Well," The Man said, showing the blank coverless front pages to John, "It appears that this book doesn't."

"But what is it?"

"Well, it's a book," The Man said, hardly turning his attention from the words.

"I know that," John said, staring at the front and back pages which were blank. "But what's it called? Who wrote it? What's it about?"

His intrigue was bordering on scathing obsession. There was no cover at all. No title and no author and no blurb. And the cover, it hadn't been dog-eared or needlessly torn, for there was not a lick of paper out of place. There was not a nick or a cut or a tiny thread out of place from the finely woven spine. It was just a book without a cover as if someone had been crazy enough to want it this way.

"I don't know what it's called," The Man said. "And I'm fairly sure I'm blank as to who authored it."

"Maybe I've read it before," John said, now desperate to know the title. "What's it about?"

"I'm not quite sure," The Man said smiling. "I suppose I'll find out at the end."

As the bus rode along, John tried to think of the last book he had read or the last film he had watched without having first read a blurb or a review. He couldn't think of one. He couldn't even think of a room he had been in at any point in his life that hadn't already been designated for some purpose.

The Man's eyes lit as he strolled over every word in a way that John had never seen another person read, different to the scores of people besides him who all courted the same novel, turning page after page in unison with one desperate person who just got on at the last stop asking, "For god's sake, does anyone know if he catches the whale?"

"What do you do?" John asked, watching how The Man mouthed the words "Oh, my!" and "Well, I never." Not as if he were doggedly following the dialogue, but as if each paragraph were a stone that hinged him further to genuine intrigue and surprise.

"I am a philosopher," The Man said.

"Where did you study?" John asked, intrigued, like a man with a swollen cyst having so luckily stumbled upon a wandering physician.

"I didn't."

John looked frazzled.

"But how can you be a philosopher if you didn't study?"

"Does a drunk have to attend a meeting to know that he has a problem?"

"Alright then. What's the meaning of life?"

"Would it really make a difference if it told you?" The Man said.

He had a look on his face as if he knew. John could tell.

"I need to know."

"You know enough already. Do you really need to know one more innocuous thing?"

"It's not nothing. It's life. Why are we alive?

"What will it change if you understand now before you've finished your own story? And what then if you didn't like the ending, would you put the book down? Would you ever pick another one up?"

"Maybe."

"But you could never understand the ending without having read the entire story and even then, it might be you who is out of context."

"Just tell me, why do we do the same thing every god damned day?"

"Existence is an equation; a series of patterns, it is one singularity, divided into an infinite number of wholes which too are further divided into infinitesimal complexity and chaotic function. There is no difference or inequality. A light can be no more on than on, and it can be no more off than off."

"What does that mean?"

"Everything is one," The Man said.

"What about people? People are different."

"A one of any colour is still a one."

"Can I change my future? Can I change the result?"

"Why not just change your expectation? It seems more pragmatic."

"I wish I didn't know how everything was going to be. I wish there was one thing that I didn't know, that I couldn't see coming. Like when I was younger and everything made sense. If this is it if this is life if I know every outcome, then why shouldn't I just kill myself now? Why isn't that the grand philosophical dilemma? If my purpose is to fulfil every expectation and if there are no more surprises, then am I omniscient? Is this how God is with mankind, with his creation, with free will? Has God hanged himself, somewhere where no one bothered to look, in the dark side of heaven?"

"Yes," The Man said, bored.

"Who are you?"

"Who are you?" The Man responded.

"I asked first."

"I am the footprint of my past," The Man said. "I am like the displacement of water, proof enough that from my past, I exist in the present and, therefore, can be gambled upon someplace in the future. I am a collection of my memories. Without them, I am someone else."

"I'm John," said John.

"I know."

"How?"

"It says so. ON your breast."

John looked down at the silver name badge hanging from his left breast pocket in plain and simple view. He wondered then, for a second, if there were two lines, or a hundred and fifty characters, written on his back that best synopsized who he was and hinted toward who or what he might become.

"Do you believe in time travel?" John asked.

"I do not see time as linear, with a zero on one side and a one on the other."

"Then what is time?"

"Something we outgrow. Something to wish and then reflect upon"

"I want to live in the present. To exist. To be. Right now. Always now."

"You cannot live in the present for you are versed only in the past."

"That's not true. Right now we are debating."

"And you are referring to something that I have already said. The moment I open my mouth and the moment I speak, as you follow my words and interpret them in your mind, you are caught on the coat tail of time, and so you are caught in the past."

"Right now," John said, "I am scratching. I'm not responding to you. I am scratching my arm. I can feel it. It is in the present."

"There is a lag between your conscious and subconscious. You are not existence. You are the expression of existence. You are the wake that trails behind the vessel of the dead. You are the expansive and fraught echo of media that terrorizes after the blood and dust have settled. Everything you think will be in reference to what has already been or in theory, what one day will come to be. But in the future, when it is perceived as being the present, you will only know it has come into being by examining it in the past."

"I've been thinking about the past a lot, like all the chances I had and if I could what I would do differently. If I could…"

"There is an equation for that dilemma. Hindsight equals foresight minus insight. You need to think about tomorrow. That's it. Nothing else. Think about tomorrow and the day after that."

"What about today?"

"You would have thought about that yesterday. It's already covered."

The bus stopped and The Man got up and squeezed past John, throwing the book towards him and smiling as he alighted through the central door. "But I might be wrong," he said.

As the bus started to pull away, John took The Man's book in his hands, flicking through the pages so that the words swam over one another like shadowy waves and he hovered over the pages, as he had when he was a boy, above the edge of a swimming pool, wanting to dive in but scared to death and unsure where to begin. He didn't even see The Man waving, before turning and walking in both directions, up and down the street.

He put the book down and stared out the window and he saw, on the sidewalk, a big red balloon that had appeared out of nowhere and was blowing down the street, in the direction of a small girl that was holding her grandfather's hand, waiting in line to buy some coloured string. The big red balloon bounced down the sidewalk and stopped at the little girl's feet. John tried to look behind, but he couldn't see where the balloon had come from. He wondered if it had been part of a celebration; a christening, a birthday party, a retirement or maybe a funeral.

The little girl, still holding her grandfather's hand, leaned down and picked up the balloon and then wobbled it around the air. Holding onto the coloured streamer that was tied to its end, she waved the balloon back and forth and giggled maniacally as it flew up in the air and then pulled back towards her, bouncing back off her hand each time.

If that balloon were a book, John would want to know what it was doing there on the street, where it had come from and who blew it up in the first place. He wouldn't play with it until he knew these things. And a strange astonishment washed over him as he watched the little girl playing with the red balloon, holding her grandfather's hand and waiting in line to buy some coloured string. Though there was no reason for the balloon being there though its presence was without explanation, it seemed that the little girl did not care, she still found fancy in its game. And the game didn't need to be defined to be fun. It didn't need to have meaning to have a purpose.

Everything in John's life was to be expected.

Everything was planned.

Nothing ever came out of nowhere.

A Brief Introduction to Active Noise Reduction

Tracy was already waiting at the stop in front of their house. She'd asked John if he'd remembered to pick up something to eat on the way back from work and he told her he'd forgotten. She said it didn't matter, but her words did little to hold back the gale of unease that rocked John's already shaky foundation. When she asked him why he didn't drive, he lied and made up some excuse about the car's distributor and when she asked him what bus he was on, he lied again.

When the bus got close to his house, John didn't press the bell. He thought about it. He even twitched his finger as if he were anxiously waiting for the right time. But the bus drove right past his house and right past his wife.

It continued in a direction which he hadn't travelled in many years, into a part of town that he hadn't seen since he was a boy. And as he stared out the window, seeing the lines of sycamore trees whose thick straggling roots, broke apart the footpath as if it were a poorly sewn seam, John's mind started to recall memories that like this part of town, he had long since forgotten.

He remembered how when he was seven, he and his friends had thought that these trees were gargantuan and wanted to climb them, and to take nest up high on the thick overhanging branches, kicking your feet and spitting on the roves of the cars that passed below, that was the greatest feat imaginable.

And though he never thought he could, he did, one day when he was all alone, climb to the highest branch that reached out over the cobblestoned street and he sat nervously on the limb, hidden beneath a canopy of green leaves, watching the cars and the people pass by underneath.

And though he knew his friends would never believe him, he told them anyway. He told them about how tiny everything seemed and about how the wind almost blew him off his perch. And he told them about a nest he saw that was literally just within his grasp and in it, the three little baby birds that were chirping and waiting for their mum to come back with food.

And when nobody believed him, he showed them a single leaf that he had picked from the highest branch to prove it but his friends all scoffed and said he was just making everything up and that no one could ever get to the top, especially not him, and that it was just a stupid leaf.

The only other time he had called this memory before today was when he first garnered the courage to talk to Tracy. He had wanted to for years, but he had neither the gall nor the confidence to approach her. To speak to her and to make her care what he had to say, for John when he was a young man, was the greatest feat imaginable.

Tracy had been sitting under the very tree he climbed when he was seven. Now, fourteen years later, he returned to that very spot and took a deep anchoring breath, as he had when he was a boy, and approached Tracy and he told her the story of when he was brave and how he climbed to the highest branch and spent the whole day, high above the earth, hidden inside a canopy of green leaves, watching over a nest of baby birds.

He spoke to her as if they had known each other their whole lives and she listened with such delicate address as if they had. He spoke about how scared he had been to leave the ground and how around his friends, he had less courage than when he was on his own but how he thought that his courage was dependent on this exact tree and none other. And Tracy listened to him telling his story and she heard and felt, in the spaces between his words, the very courage that he spoke of.

And before he left, he showed her the leaf that he had kept with him since he was a boy. And as they aged and their love grew, she kept that very leaf in a locket that she wore around her neck.

Now, staring out of the window, the trees didn't seem so gargantuan. They just looked like trees and the giant crevices in the earth where the thirsted veins of this great tree scourged through, they were less impressive than he had imagined and remembered.

They looked like more of a nuisance than anything.

And though he tried to see them in the same light, he couldn't.

And as he stared at the trees, which in his sight and now in his thoughts, seemed marginal and hardly a laudable feat, he grew a disliking for the very memory that had for years, for as long as he had stayed away from this street, seemed so full of life and colour and immense dimension and inspiration. A memory that now, as a grown man with a cynical and hollow imagination, seemed minute and trivial.

He felt tightness in his chest and a small ache in his mind. It felt as if someone was stabbing a tiny pin through his skull and his brain, and deep into his thoughts, just above his right ear. And that was where he anchored his hand, trying to equal the pressure and stop the sharp stabbing pain.

And then, as quickly as it had come, the pain went away. And with it so did the memory of having ever climbed that tree. And so too, the proof that he remembered having kept with him all those years and having given to the girl whose attention had once seemed as vast and scaling as the tree under which she sat.

As he stared out of the window, he looked at the rows of sycamore trees and the only thing he could think of, the only thing he could remember, was the scoffing and laughing and mocking of his friends. And the pain in his mind, as if someone was stabbing his imagination, it slowly eased like the dulling of a ringing in one's ear, until the memory, much like an abused frequency, faded and ceased to exist.

Eventually, John got off the bus and walked two blocks along a sprawling footpath in the middle of suburbia. Massive two-story houses with equally massive boats and yachts, moored to silver faucets and braced by red stone bricks, and two cars in every driveway, cars as big as boats. Every lawn was manicured and every hedge was trimmed and rounded and there were no fences dividing the people who walked along the path from their immaculate gardens and their front doors which by all accounts, were probably unlocked.

John strolled by and he felt somewhat foreign. Gone was the intoxicating plume of urgent conspiracy, that which silted his thoughts as he drove to and from work every morning, choking on fetid exhausts, beeping horns and clocks that were never set at the right time.

Gone too was the threat of being held up by bad traffic, flooding rain or some jackass with a replica gun, and never quite knowing the depth and severity of the puddle ahead, but always assuming the worst and waiting until the waters receded, or until the jackass got bored and turned the gun on himself.

John felt different as he walked along the path, staring collectedly at the rows of houses and feeling almost as he had felt as a young boy, walking home from school – almost, but not entirely. Just as he was disconnected from the city, no longer feeding his subconscious a diet of fear, stress and absolute dire consequence, he too was disconnected from his youth, for even then, though his troubles and burdens could be regarded as infant and minuscule compared to his now gargantuan obligations, back then, in fact at every point in his life, everything seemed to always feel ominous and pressing.

The houses were mostly the same and he remembered, as he passed them, how in some, when he was a boy, he was fearful of being mobbed and attacked by the feral children and their tattooed and nocuous parents who smoked on the front lawns and drank beer, at a time when most folks were drinking orange juice or flavoured milk; and in other houses, he imagined himself being whisked inside by the cute girl or girls that he adored and while their parents and big bully like siblings were out, having absolutely awesome, incredible sex with one, two, three, five, sometimes every single girl that he could remember from school and the movies, that he thought about in that kind of way.

As he walked past those very houses, he wondered what those girls might have become. And the feral kids too. Their houses were almost untouched, after all the time that had passed. But as he walked past, he felt neither mousey nor ravenous and he thought it a little silly, that he had ever felt that way in the past.

For now, looking into the mangled yard and watching the flickering television through the hanging wire door, he imagined himself so pacifically, as if he were merely stretching out his sleep on a Sunday morning, walking across the road, kicking down the wire door, and taking the young boy who terrified him nearly to death when he was young himself, the young boy who was now a gangly emaciated junky, and beating him to near death, until he coiled on the ground and his swollen jaw jerked and twitched uncontrollably, like a fish out of water.

"You shouldn't do it you know."

John looked around. He couldn't see anyone.

"Down here," said the voice, sounding muffled. "Under your shirt."

John pulled the neck of his shirt out and peered down at his chest. His right nipple was already on the verge of explaining everything.

"Listen, we both know you could kick his arse. There's no denying that whatsoever. All I'm saying is what good will come of it? What do you have to prove?"

"I can make him feel the way he made me feel."

"Yeah. Ok. You scare the shit out of him maybe you rough him up a bit, but you really gonna make him feel like you felt? I remember too you know. It was just him, was it? The way we felt about him, it was dependent on the way we felt about so many other things. Like the sexy girls, and the overgrown bush that we thought was full of snakes and scorpions, and the Tyrannosaurus trees that were too big to climb, and how we never had a cool pair of shoes, not once. All of it, the way we felt about everything, it was all connected like lights on a friggin Christmas tree. You take out one bulb, just one, then none of em light up. Now I don't know man, I'm just your right nipple, but I don't think we should be fucking with our past. You know? Think about it sure. Imagine it and even want, when we're laboured and chained into our boredom and repetition, but leave it at that."

"What do you think will happen?" John asked.

"I don't know," John's Nipple said, "but nothing good can

come from fiddling around in the past. Let's say you change one thing, the way you feel about the ass clown. You change that one thing, then how are you gonna feel about everything else? What are we even doing here? We should be at home, cheek to cheek, nipple to nipple with the woman we love."

"But I left something here, a long time ago. I just want to see if it's still there if I can take it back with me. I'm not looking to change anything. I know there'll be some ripple, some event, and then like everything in life, it will all even out and I'll be no different regardless of whatever change may come. My life will be paternal, consistent and empty. I'll feel like this again, no matter what. But if I could feel this one thing again…."

They continued along the road – John and his nipple - barely uttering a sound as both idly stared at the rows of houses, feeling waves of familiarity and memory wash faintly over their thoughts and senses like parched breath upon dry sunburned skin.

"Is this it?" John's Nipple asked.

"I think so" John replied.

They both stared up at the two-story house from the bottom of the wooden steps. John had the right side of his shirt pulled up so his nipple could see what he could see.

"Seemed bigger you know," John said, sounding deflated.

"I know. A lot bigger. And the steps, god the steps…"

"I could barely make it from one to the other, without falling into the gap," John said.

"Doesn't seem as scary at this time of the day."

"I only remember it at night," said John. "I don't think it's the time of day. We've just gotten older."

"You remember it well?"

"This was one of the strongest memories I had from my childhood. This house, Dracula, thinking, no, knowing, seeing and believing that Dracula was here and that he tried to eat all the children. It was so god damn scary. And the fact that you know, no mums and dads seemed to care or even know like he was invisible to adults and our screaming and our shouting, nobody could hear and nobody ever came to take us inside, to keep us safe. I really thought it was real you know."

"Shit, me too man. I was tryna jump right off your chest half the time, wondering what the hell you kept getting us into and loving it, in a weird way. I wouldn't have been anyone else's nipple" John's Nipple said, admiringly.

"This was the first time I met Tracy. Didn't really love her or anything. I was like five or something. But I remember her frizzy hair and her crazy laugh; how she'd hold her belly with one hand and slap her thigh with the other. I remember how I thought she was strange. I'd never known anyone with hair like that and with skin that colour and who smiled so wide and so often. I remember I thought she was strange, but an interesting kind of strange. I wanted to know her. I wanted to be her friend."

"She thought you were a dork."

"I know. God, it took her forever to come around."

"Whatta you say? Shall we go up?"

"I dunno," John said. "My head is still kind of sore."

"C'mon. What are ya? A Coward? Knock on the door?" John's Nipple said, egging him on.

John smiled and so did his nipple. A light wave of trepidation shivered about them as they thought about creeping up the stairs as they had done as children and edging inch by inch towards the brown oak door, John with his left hand extended to rat tat tat on the door and his right hand gripping the wooden handrail, almost catching every protruding splinter in his palm as he moved nervously, step after step.

He almost felt as he did as a boy, daring to climb the stairs and knock on the door of Dracula; just him and his nipple. He felt the same air of sudden fright, expecting the door to burst open at any second and a caped and fanged monster to soar down the steps after him, thirsty for his blood as he sprinted down the road or down an alleyway or up the stairs of his house, towards the safe and secluded corner of his bathroom, between the toilet and the tub.

When they reached the top of the stairs, John looked back to see how far he had come and when Dracula was to burst out, how far and in what direction he would have to run. When he was a boy, from the top of the stairs, the world about and the children below, they all seemed too minute and paltry. Now as a grown man, with longer legs and prescription lenses, it didn't seem so vast anymore.

And even before he lifted his hand to the door, he could feel a pain starting to swell inside his thoughts. Like the other pain, it wasn't anything that he could bandage or put pressure on. It wasn't the kind of pain that he could find. It wasn't in his bones and it wasn't in his skin or in his nerves. It was inside his thoughts and it was sharp and stabbing.

"You alright," John's Nipple asked.

"Let's just do this" replied John, the pain now searing as he lifted his hand and knocked on the door.

His heart beat fast.

His stomach sank.

He could hear the sounds of footsteps and he tried to imagine the Dracula that he had had in his mind since he was a boy; a savage beast of monolithic proportion with nails like jagged and rusted razor wire and arms as wide as a jumbo's wingspread. He could feel now as he did then, calling the memory into his conscious mind.

The air tasted the same.

His nerves were identical.

That same wave of fright pooled at that same point in his legs.

"Who is it?" cursed an old man's voice behind the brown oak door.

"Get ready to run," John's Nipple shouted.

"I said, who is it?" the voice spoke again.

John stayed still. He thought about running now, but he couldn't. He had to wait until Dracula was out in the open. And then, when the monster's long and pointed fingers were near his grasp, only then could he run. John stayed completely still, watching the door and gripping the railing.

The handle creaked as it turned.

"Run" John's Nipple shouted.

"Not yet" John shouted.

The door swung open.

"Who is it? Who are you?" the voice shouted. "Who's there? Who is it?"

And then everything became small and insignificant once more. The steps became minuscule and the gaps between them passable. And Dracula, he was nothing more than a crooked old man, hunched over his cane and shaking his angered index finger at what he thought was an intruder, merely a lock of his own hair that the wind was blowing against and tickling his nose.

He didn't at all seem scary. How the hell did he think this little man was such a gargantuan monster?

"What was I thinking?" he said, walking back down the steps with his nipple and ignoring the old man's desperate plight to shake off his tickling intruder.

"I guess when you're smaller...." John's Nipple said.

And then the pain shot straight into his thoughts and t felt as if someone had poked a skewer through his ear and into his imagination and they, whoever they were, were twisting and turning the skewer until the memory wrapped into a tight spaghetti-like bind and then they pulled the skewer out, taking the memory with it. John screamed as the pain shot through his mind as fibre after fibre was pulled from his subconscious as the memory was uprooted.

"What's happening?" he screamed.

"Don't fight it?" John's Nipple said. "Let it go."

John screamed once and then fell to the floor panting. It felt like someone had ripped every hair out of his head in one fell swoop. He clutched his hand to his head and his hair was there, but there was no relief.

"What the fuck was that?" John said, gasping for air.

"We should get home."

John and his nipple walked towards the bus stop and waited in the late afternoon sun for the bus to come. John looked back at the street and at the house which for his whole life, had been a cornerstone in his identity, a story he always talked about with Tracy, whenever he talked about their childhood and how he was, in his thoughts, so magic and fanciful.

"It's just a fucking house," he said.

"It always was," John's Nipple replied.

"No. In my head, it was so much more. I thought it was so much more. But it was just a fucking house. And Dracula, he was just some hunched-over, blind man."

John tried to think about the house and Dracula as he would any other day, remembering how he, along with scores of other boys, crept up the stairs and when nearing the door, ran screaming and sprinting down the street in a flock of chaos and swirling arms. He used to be able to remember this moment like a scene in his favourite movie, one that he liked to imagine over and over again. He used to be able to remember it, but not anymore. And as he sat on the edge of the bench, he tried to call that vision of himself as a young man but all he could see what the image of a rickety old weatherboard house and a feeble old blind man, striking at his swishing fringe.

"It's gone," John said. "The memory. It's gone."

"Good riddance," John's Nipple said. "I hated that memory anyway. We can make better ones ourselves. How ya feeling?"

"Strange."

"Good or bad strange?"

"Changed," John said.

"Was it what you were looking for?"

"It's not the feeling that I thought would be here. It wasn't what I wanted to feel."

"We can look somewhere else," John's Nipple said. "What did you want to feel?"

"I'm not sure," said John.

"Hey look, here comes the bus. We should get back home."

"You're right," John said. "You're always right."

"I'm your nipple. It's my job to be right" it said proudly.

Increment IV – licks, grooves, sweeps and tasty fills

When John arrived home, his car was in the driveway and Tracy was busy inside readying the table with pretty placemats and coloured cups and plates that matched her spacey demeanour. He paid no mind to the car or as to how it got there for, like most things in his life, there is where it always was. He opened the door and as he walked through, he stopped in the doorway for a second and peered over his shoulder, back out onto the street where people and cars, constantly pressed for time, pushed and prodded their way through and around one another, beeping and shouting and waving their pointed hands in the hair as if they were shooing mammoth mosquitos.

Then he looked back into his cramped house, the same strip of dull paint peeling off the walls, the same torn sofa they had bought when they first moved in together, still pushed into the same cobwebbed corner of the living room, the same piece of shit analogue TV they'd had all these years that only picked up static and late-night evangelism, and the small TV sitting on top that was half the size and black and white, but still, it somehow managed to suffice.

He looked back over his shoulder again and everything outside was dull and grey and forward-thinking. Everything was future driven. He pressed his foot out of the doorframe and onto the concrete in his driveway and instantly, he thought about work, but not what he had done merely, tomorrow and for every day that would follow, what he had still yet to do. He thought about bills he had to pay, about movies he wanted to see and about the places to which he would never be able to afford to travel.

He thought about projects he would deliver, milk that he would produce, people that he would have to speak to, the invitations they would give him and the excuses he would use. He thought about the weather. Not the way it was with the sun setting off the divide, but about tomorrow, how it will be and whether he should water the garden bed in the morning before going to work, or tonight, when everyone finally goes home.

Every thought was future driven.

He pulled his foot inside, onto the doorway and then every thought ceased. And then, when he pressed his foot onto the stained and faded wooden living room floor, the first thing he heard was Tracy's voice saying, "How was your day?"

He looked over his shoulder at the future buzzing about outside and then he returned to see the woman he loved, and he lost himself entirely at the faint lines under her eyes, which etched, like the warm and bumpy grooves in an old record, a passage of time that they had unravelled and shared. Some of the lines were cavernous and wounded apologies while others were infinitesimal fissures of avowing forgiveness and swallowed pride, in her soft caramel skin.

"So… How was your day?" she asked again, in the past.

Everything about her was the past; the way that she spoke, the way that she dressed (with her shuffling bare feet invisible under her long red gypsy skirt) and how she smiled, for she was always looking as if she was relieved that he was home as if every moment was one of pained and delectable yearning.

He looked behind again and he saw the future and then he looked back and embraced the past.

"What happened?" she asked.

"This door," John said. "It's a portal, a wormhole. Outside, everything is tomorrow and me, my thoughts and my mind, they are busy shaping a future, visualizing it in my mind's eye, and applying it to this canvas of the present. But it's the future. And the result of that future" he said, with a look of shock, "the job well done, it will only ever be known to me in the past."

"I didn't understand," she said.

"I don't see what's so difficult," said John's Nipple.

"Everything outside this doorway is the future and everything inside is the past. You are my history."

"I thought you said I was your future?"

"So this door…" he said, caressing the wooden frame like

an artist, their finished piece. "This door is a wormhole, a bridge between the future and the past. We are time travellers" he said, ecstatic.

"Did you get the things I asked for?"

"Fuck" he shouted.

"I thought you might forget, so I picked some things up earlier."

John followed her around the house, observing her intensely as if she were an equation that he had just noticed.

"I made this dress today," she said, spinning in a circle; the dress, lifting to show her bare naked feet.

"I always said she had talent," said John's Nipple. "Didn't I always say that?"

"You did," said John, acknowledging his nipple. "You did indeed."

"Amor, have you seen my necklace?" Tracy asked. "I took it off earlier, but I didn't come across it anywhere. Did you see it when you came in?"

"It's here," John said, picking the silver necklace up from the coffee table.

He held the pendant in his hands and unlocked it with his two stubby fingers and it was empty. The leaf he had given her when he was a young man, the single leaf she had carried close to her heart all these years, was gone.

"Where is it?" he shouted.

"Sorry. I didn't hear you" she said.

"The leaf. Where is it?"

"What? What leaf were you thinking of?" she asked confused.

"Our leaf" he shouted. "The leaf I gave you, under the tree, when we were…"

John stared at the empty pendant and then down at his nipple and then back at his wife who had since entered the room and had a look on her face as if he were talking utter nonsense.

"What leaf Amor? You never gave me a leaf."

John stared deeply at his wife, deep into her eyes and at the lines on her skin, some of which had lightened and faded and even vanished as if her skin were a balloon that had filled with an extra breath of life.

"What's happening?"

"Did you have anything to drink yet?" Tracy asked, holding up a carton of Shante Creative Milk.

"I fucking hate that shit," said John. "Milk shouldn't burn. Just, you know, milk and pepper don't mix. They shouldn't bloody mix."

"Amen to that brother," John's Nipple said.

"Oh, I told everyone to come round at six so you know…"

"What's the time now?" John asked.

"Well it was five fifty-eight two minutes ago" Tracy replied, brushing her hand lightly over John's. So light was it that John didn't even notice that her hand passed right through his, like a ghostly shadow.

Tracy wandered off into another room, preparing some snacks, drinks, and games. John watched her. He watched how she floated about like a grain of sand in a tiny puddle. He watched how her buttocks rounded and clenched as he leaned over to pick up things from way down low and he watched how her supple breasts curved and shaped like smooth and unspoiled ranges. And he watched too, how her nipples stood round and firm and erect, even when she wasn't cold or aroused. And he watched her, as he watched her every day of his life, and he felt as empty and content as he always had.

"I love you," he said, feeling nothing. "I love you," he said again, this time shouting.

"I heard you," Tracy said. "I said I love you back. I said I love you even more."

He didn't hear it, but he knew that she did. She always did. There wasn't a moment they passed one another when they didn't exchange such pleasantry; a thousand times a minute, one million times per day.

"What's wrong?" asked John's Nipple. "I can always tell

when you're down."

"Look at her," he said, lifting his shirt so his nipple could see Tracy, as her silhouette carved into the fading evening light.

"What about her?"

"That's just it. I know any other guy would die to take her out, to dine her, to dance her, to bed her, to make her cum, to make her sing, to make her shiver and shake with delight, to make her feel how she deserves to feel, how I wish I could make her feel."

"But you do. She loves you. You make her feel like that."

"But I don't feel it myself. And I don't think she does either. If she does, it's just a memory of how I made her feel in the past. It's not how she feels right now."

"But you love her right?"

"Of course I do. I don't deny that. I tell her I love her because I do, I do love her. It's just… It's been so long since I felt what our love was like, outside of fighting and almost breaking up of course. When everything is like now, calm and placid, without any fracture or worry, without any excuses or blasted apologies. I wish we didn't have to almost sever, to feel the way we did the first time."

"Then think of her as delicate, as breakable, as something finite. Think of her as an egg" John's Nipple said. "Look at her. Look at how she takes the carton from the fridge to the sink – with the utmost delicacy, as if every egg in that carton might smash and cover her and the floor in foul yellow decay. But look" John's Nipple said, standing erect on John's chest and pointing towards the kitchen counter where Tracy stood with the poise of a ballerina and the glare of a hangman. "She breaks the egg with such gentility. Even you do. I have seen you many times. All humans do, even the most brutish whose hands are all thumbs, they, like you and like Tracy, break an egg with delicate address. You need to think of her like an egg, something delicate, something fragile. You need to touch her gently as if the slightest coarse abrasion might peel away her skin. You must hold her – sure enough, to keep her safe and warm but delicate enough as if her bones were made of sand and the slightest breeze, even a heavy breath, might blow her away so that nothing of her remains. You must kiss her as if her lips were a fine crystal that might shatter in the flurry of your typical orgiastic affection. Your love was and is a universe. The second you said I love you, your heart…"

"Exploded," said John.

"The birth of a universe," said John's Nipple. "And like any universe, you fill your lives and your relationship with memories, some of them solid objects that you cling to and revolve about, and some of them dark invisible emotions that are unspoken and unseen, but are evidently there, only, for the moment, they are unprovable. And like any universe, after time, your love expands and expands until eventually, you become so distant from your beginning, that your love and your passion slows and cools."

"I want to feel that way again. I want to feel that love."

"Create another universe, a parallel plain or…."

"Or what?"

"Divide zero. Crumble the infinite fraction."

"Break up with her?"

"No. Your universe would still exist. She would become a black hole, lurking in the back of your mind, ready to consume any new joy that you encounter. You must destroy the number line entirely. You must eradicate the fibres of her being from your heart and mind. Or…."

"Or what?"

"A parallel plain. Create a new universe. And feel love again."

"How?"

"Have a child?" said John's Nipple.

John watched his wife gently crack an egg against the bowl and pull the shell apart with two fingers.

"I wish she would break me like that," he said to his learned nipple.

When he walked into the kitchen, John saw Tracy leaning over the counter, playing solitaire on her computer as eggs bubbled and hissed in the pan beside her.

"I don't know why you play that," he said.

"You used to love Solitaire," she replied.

"I just don't see the point anymore. The game is already decided before you begin. Your only purpose is to flip the cards. That's not playing, that's participation. If the outcome is not in my hands, then what's the point?"

"I haven't played it in ages. When I was young, I always chose the winning hand."

"That's what I mean. What's the point?"

"It felt good to win once in a while, and like you're saying, it was in my hands, it was my choice."

"I'm tired of knowing how everything will turn out."

"Did you wake up on the wrong side of the bed this morning?"

"Tell me something about you," John said, his voice sounding sterner, nearing desperate and shaky, almost dangerous. "Tell me something you haven't told me. A story, something about your family, about you, maybe a dumping or some stupid thing you did while drunk.....Anything, just something new, something you haven't told me yet."

Tracy smiled.

"Amor," she said, "I already told you everything about me; everything."

"Is there really nothing? No stories? Nothing at all? No more depth? No more dimension? Are you telling me I know everything about you? Your desires, your secrets, your fears, your repressions, your doubts, and indecisions, your regrets....Everything?"

"I told you everything my love, of course. Why, what did you keep from me?"

She smiled playfully as she got up from the computer and walked through John, passing through his skin like a bitter chill on an icy morning.

"Nothing," John said flatly. "Nothing."

And he was right. He hadn't kept a thing from her. They had, over the years, told each other everything; every dark and saucy secret and every deep-seeded shame and regret. There wasn't a piece of unturned soil in their marital terrain. Their universe was expansive indeed, but its very dimensions had been absolutely defined. There were no new areas to explore, there were no new shapes to take form. All that could be was.

Their love offered nothing to unravel.

Their love held no surprise.

And all of a sudden, John felt his universe shrinking.

"So all that's left," he said "is that one of us dies."

"I didn't catch that, what was it?" she shouted from the other room.

"Nothing," John said. "Just talking to my nipple."

"You love her, you do. You wouldn't feel this way, this mournful, if you didn't. All dust settles eventually. You let the barnacles of complacent satisfaction cling themselves to your nerves."

"If knowing means forgetting, then strip me of my knowledge then unlearn me so I can discover it all again."

"Do you want to?" asked John's Nipple. "You only need ask."

"What do you mean?"

"The man on the bus. He said that without his memories, he is someone else. I think what he meant is that a human is like a glass jar. Empty, it has no name and no defined purpose but once it's filled with useful or useless junk, and once it's left in a defined space, it assumes a purpose and an identity and if its contents are changed, so too are its identity and its purpose. Each person is a book and when they are born, their pages are as blank as their thoughts. They have no imagination and no title. The person's memories fill those pages and define their identity and their purpose."

"So what? I tear out some pages, erase some memories and I change the story? But how?"

"You've already started. The leaf; it wasn't in the locket."

"You know where it went?"

John's Nipple smiled.

"It never existed," said John's Nipple.

"What do you mean?"

"When we passed the Tyrannosaurus trees, you remembered when you were a boy. That memory was a chapter in your life. It was a memory of sense, one where all of the facts were clear and unchanging, one that had a feeling and a meaning, a definition, and a purpose. In your life, you have told that story a hundred maybe two hundred times, maybe more. You told it to Tracy when you first saw her, underneath that tree. You redefined that memory; an amendment to the original story, a redux of the original piece. The place was the same. The feeling was the same. Your words, as you dared to finally speak to this girl, were as nervous and jittery as your sweaty and shaking hands, that day when you decided to finally climb that tree. And the feeling, as you sat next to her as a young man, listening to her talk about her favourite bands and about the things that bugged her, was identical, as to when you were a young boy, sitting upon the highest branch, listening to the sounds that the world made, only at the height that you were. But today, when you called that memory, you met it with your adult cynicism and you painted it with your typical boring tirade. You reduced the tree and the girl to absolute insignificance. And now, you will never be able to tell the story the same way again. As such, the leaf, or your marker for that page, it doesn't exist for this is no longer a chapter in your book. It is one of hundreds of thousands of forgotten stories, memories that influence but do little to inspire. One can relive their story over and over again, but only as a metaphor for what is real and contextual in your life. But if you call a memory and it's out of context, if the way you feel has now changed, you won't just disregard the memory; you'll sever it entirely."

"So if I relive these chapters in my life, if I rewrite then I can change how I feel about my present?"

"You heard the man on the bus. You are a collection of your memories. Without them, you are someone else. Do you really want to take that risk?"

"If I am someone else then I won't feel about Tracy as I do now. If I am someone else then she will be someone else to me, and I to her. If I am nothing to her, if I play no villainous or heroic role in her story, if I haven't polluted her mind with stories, then I can feel about her as I did, before that day at the tree. If I could feel that passion and that want and desire again for just a second, it would sustain me for the rest of my life."

"But if you are not you, why would she care?"

"It has to be worth it. It has to be better than stewing here in this" John said, stuck for words. "This ordinary life."

"You could just buy her roses you know. Give her a massage every now and then. Think about when she's ready to finish for once. I'm just saying you know…" John's Nipple said, apprehensively. "What you did or thought in the past is not as important as what you are about to do and how you feel, right now."

"Fuck you," John said. "You want me to pierce you? I can't go on like this, with this cold and stagnant love, with knowing how every day is going to be, planning for the future every day and living in a fucking world that is so god damn predictable that all those plans come true. I don't want to live like that anymore. I don't want to sit in a cubicle all day spending my creative milk on some faceless corporation, never seeing or tasting the product of my own imagination. I'm sick of it."

"Listen," said John's Nipple. "While we're on the topic, cold hands," it said bluntly. "If you're gonna massage me, you know, warm up those tweaking digits of yours beforehand. It makes a difference."

"I'm sorry," John said, feeling genuine remorse. "I didn't know."

"It's fine," John's Nipple said. "But if you could…."

"Sure, of course. What about wearing mittens?"

"Ummm," John's Nipple said, shaking its head. "Chafing."

"Oh, ok," John said. "I'll keep it in mind. I promise. Now, are you gonna help me?"

"You're sure you wanna do this?"

"I want to feel that way again. I want to erase her from my story. Are you with me?"

"Well, I am your nipple aren't I?"

If the Mouth is the Asshole of the Subconscious Mind, What then of the Sound of My Thoughts?

By the time the guests arrived, John was busy rummaging through old records that had been collecting dust in a corner of the back room, between the cat's litter trays and a stack of old washcloths. He flicked through the cardboard covers manically, trying to remember the tune he had heard the girl in the elevator humming, only hours before. Whatever it was, it was here, in this pile of memories.

"Everyone arrived" Tracy shouted, leaning from the kitchen door.

"I'm coming, I'm coming. Just give me a second," John said.

"That's what you said a second ago," Tracy replied.

John's pressure was building, he wanted to break something.

"I'll be there in a second alright? Just... go be a gracious host or something" he said, speaking clearly, under the heaviness of his frustration.

As he flicked through every cover, he felt small waves of familiarity, lapping at his conscious shore. They were landmarks, great weighted spikes that he had hammered into the asperous, rocky face of his youth, that which had given him footing and secured him should he ever fall, in the mountainous ascent from boy to man; from callow and inequitable expectation to matured and dogged obligation.

And though each of these coloured and spritely titled spikes felt familiar, as he ran his fingers from corner to corner, they didn't seem like sure footing, not as much as they had when he was a boy. But he knew whatever the hell that song was that the girl in the elevator was singing, it was in here, somewhere.

And then he found it, near the end of the pile of warped and dusted vinyl, a record he hadn't heard in a lifetime since he was a young man, living life so differently than he did today; with more passion, with more exclamation, as if one day, his thoughts and his feelings and his ideas and his discoveries, as if they would account for something.

The cover was different than he imagined it; the same but different.

When he was younger, the images of human desolation and social disorder, and the scrawling illegible titles, they had more impact than they did now, and they stood out like a whore at a christening. Now, the images just looked poorly drawn and the scrawling writing, it wasn't edgy or inauspicious; it was just annoying, no more artful or dimensional than a scuff mark on his shoe.

John slowly lowered the needle, wincing as it scratched its way on the warped ends of the record. He had forgotten the sound that a vinyl made, the warm crackling and grating, like the sound of thunder rolling about worn tires as they slowly turned on a loose gravel road. And as he listened now, his first instinct was to rattle a wire or a cable or to hit at the back of the player, to fix that infernal, broken sound.

It sounded nothing like he had imagined. The drums were less like pounding Howitzers and more like the rattling of copper coins on the inside of a crushed soda can. And the guitars, how he had once thought of them sounding like a mixture of gunfire and chainsaws, sounded like an elderly cat, crying for its supper.

And he thought about his youth; about how he had draped himself in black jeans and black shirts - painted with oral obscenities of moral and social rebellion – and black steel-capped boots, the kind that could kick through the hull of a container ship.

He thought about his friends too and about how they trawled the streets each night in a sprawling net of vagrancy, looking for girls, fights, trouble, and purpose. And it seemed like back then, everything was so simple; so clear and defined; being a part of something important and having a voice where just being was all that mattered as if he was destined for something brilliant, even if he didn't have the inspiration or the motivation to do so.

As he pulled the vinyl from its plastic sleeve, he felt as empowered and in control as he had robed in black attire; taking the record, in careful exhilaration, from its cardboard case, much the same as how a junky might draw blood into their filthy yellow syringe or in how a priest might eye a young boy as he is passed his clerical collar. He could almost taste it on his lips and on his parched and aching throat.

Then he thought about Tracy, and about how she was contrary to all of that; how she was a bright burning sun to his infinite void like darkness. He remembered how, just as he loved to drown in this record, he loved just as much, to sit and listen to Tracy humming her silly folk songs, forgetting the words as she strummed on open chords.

And he was washed with an emotion that was kind and coloured white.

But then, he thought of the girl in the elevator and the song that she was humming; that very same song. He didn't know the name of it then and he didn't know the name of it now, but it was the same song and the way he felt in the elevator hearing her hum – feeling tired, despondent and insignificant, that very same feeling attached itself to the memory of Tracy, sitting in the sun, strumming on her guitar and humming away as he, from within his circle of black-clad rebellion, shivered at the sound of her trilling voice.

But now, her voice sounded ordinary and shrill. Though she looked as she always had in that very memory, her image became polluted with how he thought of her now.

And now the memory of her, it was cold and vacuous and it was coloured black.

"This is shit," he said, throwing the cover across the floor and pulling the plug from the wall. "What the hell was I thinking listening to this crap? I was an idiot."

"You were young," John's Nipple said.

"I was stupid. Everything I thought was stupid. All of it. Scrap it all" he shouted, digging his hands into the side of his head as the needle-like pain rung in the back of his mind, twisting and skewering and wrenching the memory from its place, and all those that were tethered to it; like all the times that he lay in bed after making love, with Tracy sprawled across his chest, listening to his beating heart and singing faintly, a song she would have only just made up, and with it, every memory and every dream that ever linked to the sound of her voice.

And hundreds of thousands of memories which were all so finely woven into the fabric of this one image of Tracy, sitting in the sunshine and humming that impossible to remember the song, they too went careening into John's cerebral void. As concrete pillars, they quickly turned to shifting sand and silted from his thoughts, being swept away by the storm of his matured discontent, to settle somewhere in the nether of his subconscious, where they would do little to bother or inspire.

Then Tracy popped her head through the door. She was speaking demented like, her eyes white, wide and maddening, and her hands urgently whisking at the air, as if there were some imaginary cord attached to John's chest that she was pulling on, catching his conscious vessel and pulling it back to shore before it drifted over some reclusive and inescapable horizon.

She seemed angry. He could tell, by how crooked and jagged her teeth looked as her face, lips, and tongue all contorted into unwelcoming shapes and dimensions as they sought to form pointed words of prickly offence, the kind that, like a jabbing pointed finger, served to rile one from their still, tepid boredom into the very least they could do, to suffice their social obligation.

"What are you saying?" John shouted, reading Tracy's exclaiming face like some foreign journal. "I can't hear you. I think something's wrong. Are you speaking? Are you saying something?"

It looked like Tracy was shouting now and she threw her hands in blasted forfeit before leaving the room and slamming the door so hard that it jarred shut.

John dug his fingers into his ears, scratching at the yellow wax inside.

"I'm deaf," he said, hitting the side of his head as if he were clearing water. "I think I'm deaf. Oh god, I'm deaf."

"Shut up for a second," John's Nipple said. "Can you hear me? Can you hear what I'm saying?"

"Yeah. I can hear you. What the hell is happening?"

"I don't know what you're on about. Explain to me your dilemma."

"Tracy. Her mouth was moving, but she didn't say a thing. But I know she was speaking, or shouting or screaming or whatever. I could feel the vibrations of her voice. I could see them too, like distortions of light. I could see them, for just a second. What the hell is happening to me?"

"Everything's fine John. Just keep your shit together. People will think you're crazy or something. They'll lock us up. People act funny when they're suspicious or scared."

"I'm sorry," he said, apologizing to his nipple.

John rested his knee against the door and barged his shoulder, gripping the handle so that it wouldn't fling back against the wall. As he walked out into the living room, his senses were overwhelmed with a furious buzz of people nattering, smoke billowing and lights flickering. The hallway was dark and choking and though his first instinct was to get down low and go, go, go; he kept walking towards the murky, diffusing glow of red and blue lights that painted an air of satyric debauchery. And as the smoke-filled his watering eyes, John sighed, for he knew exactly how little dimension there was and would be, inside that room. He knew where everyone would be sitting, what kind of glasses they would be drinking from and what common story was being told, which facial expression was being worn by whom.

"Why bother?" he said.

"Mini hotdogs" John's Nipple replied. "They're delicious and better than being alone, or having to take the time to get to know someone else."

"And that's it. Once I've heard every story, over and over, so many times that I can tell it myself, then what are they to me?"

"A friend."

"A friend. A story. A lover. A life. Am I to be stuck with this life for an eternity then, once it has been lived?"

"I have a name, you know," John's Nipple said. "And a story

to tell."

"I think it's best that we remain strangers. And I don't wanna disappoint, but I don't think there's gonna be any hotdogs." John said.

John's Nipple sighed, just as John had. He had expected that answer but even still, he was hoping for something else.

"And you know what I said?" Stefan asked the party, keeping them in suspense.

John entered the room and clamped his eyes for a second as he adjusted to the smoke and light which by all accounts, were fitting for some back alley drug deal or blowjob gone bad. And everyone turned to John, clapping and hooting and whistling and chanting his name. They were in the kind of hysterics that overwhelmed maddened and riled gangs of sports fans and religious zealots, yet they were only three; Tracy, Stefan, his wife Elise, and out in the backyard, harassing his cats and seconds away from tearful willowing, his three children; The Accident, The Apology, and The Happy Ending.

"Sit down here good buddy," Stefan said tapping on the empty seat beside that both he and Tracy had no doubt prepared.

He looked at Tracy who was sitting on the floor with her legs curled and tucked under her buttocks so that it looked like she didn't have any. John stared at her, imagining that she had flowered from that very patch of Earth where she always sat when they had guests over, between the two yellow armchairs and the front door; close enough to John's seat so she could reach out and touch his knee whenever the conversation turned to the things he was working on or the plans that they had for the future, and close enough to the door so that she could hint towards it, when it was time for her guests to leave.

"We're gonna order pizza," Stefan said.

"Fuck" John's Nipple shouted, though, under the heavy jumper, nobody heard except for John.

"What flavour do you want," Tracy mouthed though no sound came out.

"What?" John said, erratic, and a little worried. "What did you say?"

Tracy looked at him oddly and again she spoke.

"What flavour do you want?" she mouthed again.

And again, her lips moved and bent into the shape of those words, and from her mouth, again the light in the air seemed to bend and warp, as if, like a black hole, the sound of those words crept about, silent and conspicuous, through the thick smoke and heavy expectant stares. John stared at her wildly, as if the wider his eyes were and the closer he stretched, the more sense she might start to make.

"What did she say?" he asked, slithering the words down his vest.

"Keep your shit together brother," John's Nipple said. "She asked what flavour you want."

"Of what?"

"Pizza," John's Nipple said; thinking of bite-sized hot dogs.

John stared back at Tracy. She was smiling, but she was asking him something. He didn't know what exactly, but he could guess. There were after all, only so many words and expressions that they had in their dialogue. They talked about the same things day after day and forever in the same lexical manner, for the things they did never changed, and neither did the bank of their vocabulary. And so when she stopped talking and he was sure it was his time to speak he said, "Whatever you like."

"Play it cool," his nipple said, urging him to sit down.

"You want a drink good buddy," Stefan asked, already pushing a glass of whiskey into John's face.

John took the glass obligingly and smiled at the room as he sat down on the armchair. Already Tracy was squirming on her folded legs, smiling proudly and seconds away from reaching her hand towards his knee, before telling some story from John's past that she assumed she had told a hundred times before while Elise and Stefan listened politely, pretending that they hadn't.

"You're not gonna believe what I got?" Stefan said, reaching into his jacket pocket.

John had stopped imaging responses to Stefan's inquisitions years before. His trained but unfelt instinct was to stretch and contort his face as if a spider had fallen onto his knee. It did the job of sufficing friend-like obligation and offered no suspicion to his actual disinterest. From his pocket, Stefan pulled out a long and thin, white joint.

"Got it from one of the guys in Marketing. They're always smoking. It's supposed to be the shit. Later on, we'll light it up, like old times, and listen to that new Nine Inch Nails song. That will be fucking shit hot. What do you think?"

John took the spliff from Stefan's hands and held it under his nose. He hadn't smoked in such a long time. He ran it back and forth under his nose, smelling the finely pressed weed, until, in a second, his thoughts slipped backwards in time, away from the sleazy lights and engulfing smoke, when, as a young man, as he gingerly rolled a dried mash of tobacco and sweet crystalline weed into a tight joint, his attention was cordoned rapaciously, by the passing of a beautiful girl with a scent like lemon tea. And immediately he stopped what he was doing, not out of will, but out of complete lack of function.

"You alright there buddy?" Stefan asked, reaching for the joint that had fallen to the floor.

John said nothing. His thoughts were still with Tracy, as she had been before time had soured her complexion and before age had bruised and withered their lust and passion. His every sense felt as clear and as transparent now as they did back then as if there was no way that he could hide how he felt, regardless of how deeply he furrowed his brow or how mean and ill-spirited he bargained his face to become.

He followed her then, in his thoughts.

He followed her onto a bus that was going in the other direction and then he followed her down the aisle and he sat two seats behind; seeing and listening through the colour of her aroma. Then, when the bus stopped and she got off, he followed her through a maze of corridors and winding stairs; up until the top of an incredible tower and then back down again. He followed her into a score of boutiques and a handful of stores, then followed her into every queue and then out of every door.

He followed her through a busy arcade and into the bustling thoroughfare, drawn by the scent of lemon tea, briskly walking and defiantly pushing through a collage of spruikers and buskers and beggars galore, desperate not to lose her; but not so much himself.

He followed her.

He followed her until she disappeared behind a flock of tourists, all dizzy with delight and historical parallax. Still wet on her scent, he followed her blindly into the square of performers and preachers and the homeless with placards. He followed her further and further until her trail weakened and he fought to push through the slurry of people to again catch her scent once more. He followed and he followed until, desperate and delirious, he tripped on a child that was being chased by its mother, through the pleated legs of buggered and bothered business attire. He hopped onto one foot and the other, and then when he lifted his head again to the busy sidewalk, she was gone.

In his thoughts, he stood in the doorway of a small store that sifted a blend of strange soul charming instruments with an endless trail of incense that coursed over his head and into the afternoon air. And as he looked into the expansive crowd, he watched as the impossibility of finding the girl, swarmed about him like high heeled, pinstriped locusts.

There was nothing but lemon tea; the sting of her scent tickling his senses.

But now, as his eyes drew upon the woman he loved, his senses were awash with that very same fragrance, the perfume that she wore every day; like sweet lemon tea. Only now, the scent was soiled with a musky air of stagnancy that hung around his thoughts like the smell of decade-old sex; in the carpets, bedsheets and in the cracks of the poorly plastered walls of any old dank and windowless brothel.

It was no longer sweet and enamoured. It was the scent that greeted him every day when he arrived home from the job that he reviled, to the squalor of a house that he had barely the income to acquire or the time, energy or the basic want to improve. It was the scent that grounded him; that earthed him from his fanciful thoughts; that never let him escape for long enough to imagine a better way to live or another way out. It was the scent that greeted him every morning with tired scorn, as moping heads narrowly missed one another, shuffling about and banging cupboards unnecessarily. It was the scent that wafted by as he struggled to piss, staring in the mirror and practising how to smile, wink and nod; and seeing what it looked like when he said things like 'I love you', 'I don't have the time' and 'No it's ok, I don't mind coming back'. It was the scent of age and confusion, looking at himself in the mirror, still expecting to see a young man but finding only the deep-set lines of remorse chiselled into his sunken face, as if, in the times between struggling to piss in the morning, and in the evening, feigning to fall asleep, his soul was being hollowed out and his body, caving in on itself.

John stumbled out of the store, knocking over a stand of exotic spices and lemon-flavoured teas; the boxes bursting open and glazing his senses. And an old man screamed.

"Hey, you. You dumb fuck. You fuck my store. I fuck you."

John turned and saw an angry and loosely versed old man with thin hair and a crooked eye, shaking his left fist and shouting obtusely as he scoured through his change drawer, desperately looking for a knife or a gun or the handle of a broom.

The desire to follow was now the need to run away.

The smell of lemon tea had him gagging, reflecting upon all of the compromises he had made; every stone that he had left unturned on his own unbeaten path, so that he could spend not nearly half a lifetime, in understanding her. He no longer remembered the reason he was in that store that day, but instead, the reason that he ran out and with it, the thousands of times in his life he had neither the focus nor the patience to finish what he had started. He remembered the cursing Chinese man, throwing clouds of coloured salts and lemon tea in his eyes as he kicked his knees and threatened to call the police. He remembered the passersby all laughing and pointing and shaking their heads in disapproval. And from that memory, he remembered all the times his mother and his father had done the same; all the times he had let them and the people that mattered and depended on him, down.

Lemon tea; it was the contrary to curious lust; it was the scent of disappointment.

"You know what I love?" Stefan asked.

"Pizza" shouted the room in merry astonishment, like a nursery of infants, discovering their own feet.

"Pizza," Stefan said in concordance, gnashing his teeth and making a horrible slurping sound as he nodded and chewed, pushing the extremity of all that he could encompass at one time. "Am I that obvious?"

"Yes," John thought, staring at Stefan as he extracted thick wedges of pizza dough and pepperoni from the gaps in his teeth, knowing too well that at any second, the conversation would coil back to work, his kids or something from last night's news.

"I don't know why we bother," John's Nipple said as both stared at Stefan hoeing down on slice after slice, drenching the clumps of sauced, cheesy dough with lukewarm beer and spoonsful of strawberry ice cream. As he chewed, his mouth convulsed - both as a grating and shovelling object and as a device of audible projection.

He bit and he chewed and he slurped and he gulped and....

"Ahhh yeah baby, Ummm, oh yeah" he moaned, licking his fat lips. "That hits the spot. "Now," he said, rightly, "you know, the real problem with terrorism is..."

And before he could highlight his point or even introduce a subject, he was shovelling more food into that swill bucket of a mouth, swallowing whole chunks of steaming pizza as his tongue fought through the gooey residue to form words and decipher the flavour of whatever the hell he was piling into it.

"God, just look at him," John's Nipple said with a certain air of disgust, revile and wondrous appreciation.

Stefan was discoursing and chewing and biting and swallowing; doing many things at once, and whilst leaning to his left to appear to validate a point, he farted, low, deep and wet; tormenting his wife who rolled her eyes subtly and didn't miss a beat as she hammered onto Tracy about the rigours of afternoon spin classes, that terrific meme she saw about being a mother of three that you'd have to have three kids to really understand, but that was still hilarious and great fun regardless, and in noticing Tracy's fledging attention, a list of facts she had learned about Coca-Cola, AIDS and koala bears.

"I don't know what's worse," John's Nipple said. "His mouth or his arse. Does he always talk this much shit?"

John stared at his friend whom he had known his whole life. He tipped his head sideways like an attentious but confused puppy, and he nodded. "Always," he said. "Everyone, always."

"There is absolutely no content in what this guy is saying. I mean nothing" John's Nipple said, looking up at John. "Your opinions stink," he shouted, in the direction of Stefan.

It didn't matter, though, just as Stefan couldn't hear the quarrelling springs beneath his flatulent buttocks, he too couldn't hear the pleas of 'Oh God' and 'Shoot me now' from beneath the cloud of both John and his nipple's heavyset squall.

"Nobody knows this fact, just me," Stefan said, almost choking on a pointed edge of thick crust. "Not the news, not the university ones, not even the…"

He went on and on and on.

"I hate you," John's Nipple said. "But I hate myself for expecting any different. Look at him John, how he eats that spoiled garbage. Look how he shovels into his gullet. He doesn't even chew. What is that?" John's Nipple asked, watching Stefan picking crumbs, crème, soot, ash and the corners of magazines from under his tongue and the crevice-like gaps in his teeth. "Is that? Pizza, beer, peanuts, jelly doughnuts, Time, The fucking Economist, Newsweek, BB fucking C, and oh god, look at that, oh no he isn't, yep he is, he's washing that tripe down with Rolling Stone. Jesus. What's wrong with you man?" John's Nipple shouted. "Don't you know what you're doing to your insides? That shit will give you haemorrhoids."

John turned to Tracy. He stared at her. He couldn't hear a word she was saying, but he didn't have to, for whatever it was, she would have said a thousand times already, and before the end of the night, she will have said it a thousand times more.

The other two he could hear; Stefan and his wife. It was hard to ignore them. It wasn't their low take on morality, race or gender indifference that was obnoxious and lamenting; it wasn't so much the kind of words they used, it was how they used them. Their words were like the panting of a stranger's warm and musky breath, against the back of his neck on a cramped and crowded train. Their ideas reeked like that stranger's blistered and bunioned feet, having dredged through the stale and malodorous footprint of popular opinion. Their mouths were instruments of educated belching.

Tracy was talking about the movie they watched last week. He could tell by the way she dipped her head when she spoke and in how she squinted her eyes. It was her philosopher's face. Whenever she talked about movies she had watched, books she had read or political messages she had seen, scrawled along the sides of freeway overpasses, Tracy tensed her face and her words became rigid, little, rounded opinions. He knew exactly what she was going to say next. He always did. He watched her mouth flapping like a broken wing and when the timing was right, he said the word 'blue'.

The whole room erupted in laughter. Stefan and his wife cheered and gave each other high fives while Tracy leaned forwards proudly, her ghostlike touch, passing invisibly through John's knee as she mutely declared her love for him with the other two both dolefully agreeing, how darling and dear that it was, how they finished one another's sentences.

"I love you," she mouthed.

"I love you," John mouthed back, matching her silence, and feeling nothing. "I love you" he mouthed again, trying to string some feeling to the end of his words. "I love you, I love you, I live you, I laugh at you, elephant shoes."

Nothing.

His words were like deflated balloons, strung from a ceiling. And though she seemed to understand what they meant, the look in Tracy's eye was no different to how she greeted other innocuous truths without wonder; like in how the number three was both the succession and the accumulation of its predecessors or in how the presence of the moon alone proved that she was fact, a space alien, hurtling through dark expanding omniverse.

"I'm starving," John's Nipple said. "You gonna stare at what's her face all night long or you gonna help me out here?"

"Shit," John said. "You're right. I'm sorry. What flavour do you want?"

"What is there?"

"Ham and pineapple, Supreme, and Stroganoff."

"Stroganoff? What the fuck man?"

"I don't know. I haven't had it before. It's Tracy's thing you know? She orders it every time, to be different. You don't wanna try it?"

"I didn't say that" John's Nipple exclaimed.

"How many slices?" John asked, reaching through Tracy to get to the box behind her.

"Two," John's Nipple said. "Before that fat bastard finishes it off."

John took the pieces and while Tracy continued to silently talk away, he lifted his shirt and fed the two slices of Stroganoff Pizza to his nipple which had a ravishing hunger.

"Wow," Stefan's wife said, holding the back of Tracy's arched hand to her face. "That smells scrumptious." She then turned to John smiling, as if she were impressed by his extravagant taste.

Tracy was looking at him and speaking. She ignored Stefan's wife, who was still holding her hand, and though there was no sound coming out of her mouth, John knew exactly what she was saying. He smiled, as he always did and when he felt like she was about to finish her story, he pretended to blush because that was one thing that she liked. But then right at the end, when her fable was done, when Stefan and his wife were poking and jeering like rowdy pirates, he pretended to get mad, riled a deranged; only settling down when she smiled playfully and reached for his tempering hand because that was how she liked her men. That was what most turned her on.

"Hot, hot, hot, hot, hot," John's Nipple shouted.

John looked down and he could see his nipple flaming red.

"Bloody drink" it shouted.

His reaction was instant. John took a glass of ice-cold coke and poured it down the inside of his shirt, sighing with relief as his nipple gulped every last drop.

"I have something to show you," Stefan said.

He sounded secretive as if he'd been planning this day his whole life but if he had, if this were his crescendo, then tomorrow, this would all start over again.

"You're gonna love this," he said.

"If I had hands I'd make a fist and punch him," John's Nipple said.

John wondered for a moment if something unforeseen might actually occur if he might feel as unexpected as many, many repetitions ago. He tried not to imagine what it could be, but it was so hard; he had spent a lifetime shaking parcels and flipping to the last pages to quell his feline curiosity. But still, there was hope tickling at the back of his mind, and on any other day he might have thought it was a tumour, but this evening, as he sat on his sofa, feeding his nipple pizza and coke, and pretending to hold his wife's ghostlike intangible hand so as not to cause her or his guests much-unneeded alarm.

"Girls," Stefan shouted.

He clapped his hands like the drunken ringmaster that he was, forcing his children to line side by side and wait for his merry command.

"The eldest," he said, slurring his speech. "She's been... She's doing that.... They do this dance thing and she's.... She's gonna be a professional like Madonna or that other one you know, that thinks she's British as well. Fuck it. Girls, do that... Do that thing you know?" he said, his head listing like a breached hull, his right arm waving around a limp wrist as if it were a broken limb on a squat, decrepit shrub.

The girls all looked awkward and embarrassed, as did Stefan's wife and Tracy, who wore the same wretched 'shit-eating-grins', unable to stop the madness and unwilling to turn away.

"What happens next?"

John's Nipple asked.

"One of the girls trips," John said. "The middle one, nobody notices except her; and she's devastated. Stefan continues to egg on the eldest, throwing his clenched fists about in small commanding circles, as if he were racing a small pony down the home straight. The wives ogle the youngest and they use such expected terms as, 'How cute' and 'Would you ever?" All the while, the middle child continues to muddle the timing and mix up her feet. Eventually, the performance finishes without much event. Stefan tells me it's because of the angle or slant on the floor. Then he says I should really come over during the week to see it on an even floor. Then Tracy gets offended because she thinks a flat floor is a metaphor for being properly grounded and she assumes Stefan has made a crack at her, pushing forty; and still no children. It gets awkward so the kids go back out onto the porch. The eldest lights a cigarette and attempts to fan away the evidence whilst the youngest points an accusing finger. The middle girl sits on an empty straw basket and she draws her nail across the creases lines on her wrist."

"You know it all so well."

"I've seen it so many times. I know when I'm supposed to laugh and sigh and the place for every oooh and aaah. I just.... I can't remember when I stopped laughing when I stopped being affected, and when it all just became so... Comfortable. "

All of these things occurred. They acted out before John and his nipple in a foggy blur. Both watched on, neither entertained nor bored. Every now and then, to the delight of his nipple, John mouthed out some of the dialogue.

"My life," John said, "is three hundred words."

"What's your favourite one?" John's Nipple asked.

"Huh?" replied John.

"Nice. Can't really think of any that I love per se. I guess I'd have to go with phallic. Makes me think of ancient Egyptians, like Xerxes or Ra or something. Come to think of it, you know with their bald heads and sturdy physique, they actually looked like giant penises so I guess it's fitting. I hate the word pretentious though" John's Nipple said, angrily.

"Why?"

"It's not the word per se, as much as how it's used and the type of person who uses it, you know? The word itself is beautiful on the ear and just as much to say. It feels like kissing a person's moist and supple attention. It's just, the word is like a gun backfiring. You know, it just seems like the type of person who would use it, wouldn't normally use a word like that every day. Maybe that kind of person would be more likely to defame with a word like 'assclown' or 'dickhead', but for the sake of fighting monsters or whatever, they have to be just as swanky and hyperbolic to get their message across. I just feel that the use of the word pretentious is, in fact, pretentious. Hearing the average twit use this word, it shits me. It's like seeing some pretty girl under the arm of some tattooed jerk."

"You say per se a lot."

"Does that bother you?"

"It just seems unnecessary is all, but it's fine. I hate the word sorry. I hate the way it makes every problem go away and makes no one responsible. I hate the way you can say words without actually feeling them and that people trade this currency as if it's legal tender. I hate the way words like 'I'm sorry' and 'I love you' and 'it won't happen again' are passed around like bonds or promissory notes, you know. The idea of communication is to say what you feel, not to leave it up to the other person to spark their own feeling. It's like giving some kid a bag of balloons on his birthday and telling him or her to blow them up. The word is a vessel. It's coding, that's all. But there has to be something to code. There has to be some content; some substance. You can't just say 'I love you', 'I'm sorry', 'It doesn't matter' or 'There's nothing wrong'. You can't. I don't hate words" John said. "I hate the lazy, conspicuous and ambiguous use of words."

"I hate the word hip," John's Nipple said, spitting as it did. "It's a god damned body part, not a way of life."

"I hate hipsters," John said.

"And hippies," replied John's Nipple.

As they debated, Stefan was busy bruising his thumb, flicking through channels on the television, unsure which of the movies he had already seen a hundred times over, he wanted most to watch again.

"Oh, I love this one" Stefan shouted.

There was that word again; love. John looked over at Tracy. She was smiling, or so it seemed. It was hard to tell on account of her having no solid form. And though he probably knew exactly what she was saying, staring at her and hearing only her breath escaping from her mouth, he couldn't tell if she was being cynical or enthusiastic, her two usual ways in how she felt about most things.

"The ending is fantastic. You never see it coming. It's always a surprise, no matter how many times you see it. Let's watch it."

"Great idea," his wife said.

Tracy agreed, saying exactly that, but her voice was mute so she looked almost as if she were mocking her friend. John laughed hysterically and everyone turned to him oddly.

"You ok buddy?" Stefan asked. "You're acting a little weird."

"Yeah," John said, composing himself. "It was just something my nipple said."

They watched the movie and when it was done, they watched one more. The whole time, Tracy leaned on John's leg and talked about her touchy boss and the fact that she had killed every single plant she had tried to look after since she was a girl. She was convinced they were connected somehow. John always thought it was her way, though, of distracting herself through the seamless repetition of ordinary events in her life.

Stefan, on the other hand, was flexing his muscle, trying to impress the girls, John and himself, by showing how versed he was in the past, saying each line of dialogue a second before the actors on the screen did; annoying the hell out of John who at this point, was daydreaming about black holes and circular saws.

"Fuck it," John shouted, jumping from the seat and almost bowling over the children who looked thankful for any kind of distraction. "I can't watch this shit. Not again. You know what I wanna see?"

The others shook their heads.

"Where is it?" he said to himself, scouring through old video cassettes, hundreds of inane videos he had collected over the decades, looking for one in particular that he hadn't seen in even longer. "Here it is," he said, pulling out an old cassette with a tattered black and white cover depicting an awful looking man with strange concerning hair.

"Is this what I think it is?" Stefan asked, slightly nervous.

John didn't reply. He just sank into his chair, pulling his legs up against his chest and curling up into a ball like he always did when he was alone. He could see Tracy mouthing the words, 'I hate this movie', but it didn't matter, not like she had supposed it would.

"Maybe we could do something else; Scrabble or something," Stefan said.

"Shut the fuck up," John's Nipple replied.

As the room flickered - a delusional-like black and white - John thought about how this movie had made him feel like a young man. It had since he was a boy, defined him. The mere mention of its title would cause looks of concern and idyllic wonder in others and a sense of purpose, direction and belonging in him. And it was a movie that he had spoken about more times than he had actually seen. Most people had; in the company that he kept of course.

He remembered it having an allure of the strange and the surreal; being both siren and obnoxious; patently obscure. And like Tracy, it was so uncommon and difficult to find and more so, to understand, amidst the barrage of popular films with their common protagonists and linear plots. It was how he had felt about Tracy, and like her, there was nothing on Earth he wanted more than to sit in a quiet, dark room and be dumbed and bewildered by its flickering glare.

But as one scene rolled into the next, John started to distance himself from the definition he had had in his mind this whole time. His first thought was, "This is shit."

It was nothing like he had first imagined. The acting was terrible, the cinematography was lazy and the editing was neither surreal nor obscure, it was merely poorly executed. And then his second thought was, "What the hell was I thinking."

He then reverted back to his first thought, "This is shit."

He fast-forwarded frantically through the film, trying to find the scenes that he remembered as being poignant, like the first time that he kissed Tracy; when he was too scared to open his eyes, letting his arms flail lifeless beside his body, fearful that should he touch her demure waist, she might crumble as if she were made of sand or his fickle imagination. Or the first time that he saw her naked body and he found himself in muted disbelief at how lucky he was, hoping that he could spend the rest of life as had been at that moment, bastille in venerating wonder of her beauty; brushing the faint shadows that crept across her breasts and into the curve of her navel with the cusp of his sight as she undressed neath the heady glow of the evening sun.

He found that scene though and his wonder and animation, as he had always attributed to this memory, turned into stale bewilderment. And in his thoughts, he remembered himself young in his feet, his teeth, and his thoughts; and he remembered, not the first time he had seen the movie, but the first time he had seen Tracy; the first time they had seen each other; as companions, lovers, and friends.

And it was as if he had discovered a wild weed in his garden, having for the life of him thought that it was some exotic flower. And as he stared into that memory, he was without wonder and without awe. He stared at her bare breasts as if he were staring at his own worn expression. In his memory, he stared at his wife's naked body as he did now whenever she rose from her slumber, bitter and scorned, cursing the morning and his attempts to lighten her mood. He stared at her naked body with the same normal disregard as he did every day following, as she soaped her body under the steaming douche, complaining about traffic, her asshole colleagues, the idiot in the apartment above who insisted on wearing high heels at 6 am, her mother, his snoring, the budget, whether or not they'd be able to make the car payment, and her chronic constipation. In his memory, he stared at her naked body, thinking of it how he thought of it now. And like any strong and effective corporate branding, after years of impressions, now and in his memory, when he saw her naked body, he didn't feel lustful, considerate and lucky; he felt, as he followed the shadows across the curves in her soft, pert skin - oppressed, inutile, financially despondent and ridden with nagging guilt; mainly because he could shit on cue.

He took the memory in his strangling grasp and he heaved it into his sub-conscious, tearing the thought of her from the fertile garden of his imagination and with it, every memory he had of her body and her face, and with that, every trial and error, every struggle and conquest and every sobering failure that had come from knowing her, from being with her every day, and from loving her.

He screamed wildly.

"What's wrong?" Stefan shouted, already off his seat, shaking his friend, as if that would loosen him of the grip of insanity.

John screamed once more, lifting his shirt and shouting at his nipple. His sight blurred as the room spun out of control.

"What's happening?" he shouted to his nipple.

He shouted again, louder and louder, but his nipple wouldn't respond.

Tracy was shouting something. She was angry and upset, but John couldn't tell. He couldn't hear a word she was saying on account of her being so mute. And an hour ago, that wouldn't have mattered, for whenever she got like this, in a fit of absolute rage, her face would look as it did now, with her lips trembling like they were as if some enormous quake at her centre were shaking her rigid, ire core to a liquefied, snivelling mess.

Normally it wouldn't matter except that, although she was shouting so desperate and furious, so dire, doleful and sore, there was no way that John could tell, no way at all; for she had no form, no shape, no colour, and no image. She wasn't there at all.

And as Stefan's wife fought to comfort her, it looked only to John as if she were comforting herself for there was nothing and nobody in her arms at all. She had vanished, she had gone, and the room would not stop spinning.

"It's gonna be ok," Stefan shouted.

John could hear a voice, faintly, but he couldn't see anyone whatsoever. He was alone in the room; in the room that wouldn't stop spinning.

"What do we do?" Stefan's wife asked.

Stefan looked at Tracy. She stood in the corner of the room catatonic, watching her husband and her lover, her partner, and her best friend, in the fit of some psychotic breakdown.

"Call an ambulance," she said, breaking from her trance and running to her lover's aide.

She knocked Stefan away and took John's convulsing hands, squeezing them tightly as she had, every other time they passed through trouble and struggle in their lives; through his constant illness which caused them so much financial strain, and through the tyranny of his depressions and his anxieties, as she fought time and time again to make him feel for himself, how she felt about him and to cast off whatever idyllic wonder and delusion he had spelt upon her body and her face; whatever inane belief he had that he wasn't good enough or smart enough or creative enough to be with her; to rid him of the thought that one day, she would rid herself of him.

The siren was loud and waling as the ambulance rushed up the street. The banging on the door felt like it could have been pounding on her own failing heart as Tracy clung to her husband and her lover, feeling him slipping away from her warm touch. She felt as if she were nursing a stranger through a fit or seizure.

The door burst open and the paramedics rushed in.

"Is this him?" they asked. "Has he had any drugs? Has he been drinking? How long has he been like this?"

"His whole life" replied Tracy, shaking like a leaf as the paramedics lifted him onto a gurney and strapped down his violent and convulsing body.

"Is he lucid?" asked one of the paramedics.

"Sort of. He just started screaming just now and this convulsing. He's also been talking to his right nipple for the past week or so" Stefan said.

The paramedics lifted John's shirt. His right nipple was pasted in tomato sauce, mustard, and chunks of pepperoni, chicken and pastry crust.

"He has pizza on his nipple," said one paramedic to the other. "Some pretty bad burns here."

"Are you the wife?" one of the paramedics asked Tracy.

"I am," she said. "He hasn't been taking his medication."

"Does he have a history of illness?"

"He was doing so well," Tracy said, bursting into tears. "I really thought this time would be different. I thought he'd..."

Stefan's wife embraced her and the two women wept as Stefan helped the paramedics load up the gurney and take John away. As the ambulance, with its flashing red lights and screaming siren, disappeared into the night, Tracy wiped away her tears and took a long, deep breath.

"Now what?" Stefan asked.

"We try again," Tracy replied, hopeful.

A Bushel of Salt

John woke the next morning, heavy-headed from the sedatives. He woke to the sound of muffled voices from the other side of the door. It sounded like the mad ramblings of a museum curator, gleefully detailing the hospital's latest exhibit; his symptoms, his history, his prescribed treatment and quietly, so as not to arouse discomfort or appear to be gossiping, pointing out the oddly mannered, shapely woman with strange obnoxious hair, in the corner who was preparing medication into cups and piling faeces-stained sheets into laundry hampers.

"She's his wife," The Doctor said to his students.

"Is she a nurse here?" the most astute of the students asked.

"Yes, she is. In fact, it was here that they first met and where they fell in love. Fourteen years ago if I'm correct." The Doctor said.

"Is that even permitted?"

"It isn't 'not' permitted per se. In certain circumstances, who am I to stand in the way of love?"

"You're a medical practitioner. You're pragmatic. So you can stand in the way of love."

"I am just a voice of reason," The Doctor said "Per se."

"Is this in the test?" a student asked.

The Doctor shrugged his shoulders. As he walked to the next room, the students took turns peering into the glass window at John who was rousing from a medicated stupor, shaking his head and looking mean and uncomfortable, back at the face through the glass.

"Come along," The Doctor said. "Don't dilly daddle."

The students all followed, leaving John alone on his mattress.

"Good morning Tracy," The Doctor said.

"Good morning sir," she said back.

"I really thought this time he would make it you know? How

long was it? Six months? A year?"

"We had twenty-one days doctor."

"My god that is impressive. That is progress. You are a wonderful and dedicated wife, a diligent and inspiring nurse and you are a good person. You should be proud of yourself. We will make him better you know, we'll find a fix to this memory problem of his."

"I'm sure we will doctor," Tracy replied.

When the doctor and his students left, Tracy wheeled her cart towards John's room and stared through the window at the man sitting on his bed. She had seen him like this, scores of times, and she would see him like this, many scores of times more; until her love was strong enough to keep him rooted in her heart and her, in his thoughts and his memories. But it hurt her to see him like this, to feel as she felt but for his touch to be so cold and foreign.

"Hi, John. It's time for your medication," she said.

She wheeled the cart to the bed and sat down beside him, resting one hand on his leg.

"My name is John?" he asked.

"It is. Do you know where you are John?"

"Is this a hospital?" he asked.

"It is John. This is a hospital John and you are a patient. Do you know who I am John?"

John looked confused. He stared at her as if she were a corner he had never turned.

"Are you a nurse?" he asked.

"I am," she said. "My name is Tracy. And I'm your nurse" she said, hinting at nothing more.

"My head is sore," John said, pressing his face against her shoulder.

Tracy rested her hand against the back of his head and slowly caressed his hair.

"We've been through worse baby" she whispered, so softly that he couldn't hear. "Please hold on. I love you so much" she said, a single tear, escaping from the crux of her tightly shut eyes and landing on John's arid lips.

When she left, John stretched the cramping from his body and walked up to the window. As he watched as the nurse wheeled her cart around, ignoring the cursing and agitated pointing of crazed patients and impatient doctors, he noticed how different and unlike the other nurses she was; how her crazy hair sprung up and down all wild and free like an untrimmed hedge, and how her skin glimmered in a certain way that made him think of how the shadows shaped themselves inside his room when the sunset through the backs of the sycamore trees that grew in the field by the window, outside of his room.

He watched her as if she were the only person that existed as if it were just him and her. The desire to be close to her, to hear her voice shivering the jittery nerves, was overwhelming. He wanted to touch her hand and feel what it was like to make her shiver, to feel the tiny bumps running under his fingers. He wanted to press his face against her neck and smell once more, the light drizzle of lemon tea that aroused from her soft skin. He wanted to stare at her forever, as she was and be still in amazement that such beauty existed.

He wanted to be a part of her world.

He wanted her to be a part of his.

He wanted to know everything about her.

And never tire.

And never be alone.

He wanted this feeling to last forever.

Also by C. Sean McGee:

A Rising Fall (CITY b00k 001)
Utopian Circus (CITY b00k 011)
Heaven is Full of Arseholes
Coffee and Sugar
Christine
Rock Book Volume I: The Boy from the County Hell
Rock Book Volume II: Dark Side of the Moon
Alex and The Gruff (a tale of horror)
The Terror{blist}
The Anarchist (or about how everything I own is covered in a fine red dust
Ineffable
London When it Rains
A Boy Called Stephany
Happy People Live Here
The Inscrutable Mr Robot
The Case Against God
The Parasite
Faraday's Cage
Harrold with an E
Alex and The Gruff: Dawn of The Bully Hunter
Self-Titled

StalkerWindow:

http://c.seanmcgee.blogspot.com
http://www.goodreads.com/c_sean_mcgee

Printed in Poland
by Amazon Fulfillment
Poland Sp. z o.o., Wrocław